The Secret Bride Society

By

Amanda Tru

Walker Hammond

Publishers

The Secret Bride Society, Book 1
Copyright © 2016 by Amanda Tru

Cover Design by Debi Warford
Images: ©
Julenochek| Dreamstime.com – The Beautiful Young Woman in a Wedding
Dress, ID 20274437
Watkins, Carleton E. | Secret Town, Trestle from the West, Public Domain

All scripture quotes or references are from the King James
Version of the Bible.

Published by Walker Hammond Publishers
ISBN-13: 978-0-9981054-13
ISBN-10: 0-9981054-1-4
Also available in eboook publication

PRINTED IN THE UNITED STATES OF AMERICA

Chapter 1
1870

"Shhh! She's coming this way!"

Leah's feet stopped. Slowly, she looked around, trying to distinguish who was watching her from the dark shadows of night.

Leah Barton was a sensible woman. Too sensible to deny that the hoarse whisper came from the darkened graveyard, and too sensible to believe that it originated from one of the cemetery's regular inhabitants.

Instead of continuing on toward the safety of the church, she boldly stepped toward the tombstones lifting their white heads in the light from a nearly full moon.

"Who's there?" she demanded, refusing to let her voice quaver even a little. She had three younger siblings. Her firm voice could evoke repentance from the sneakiest transgressors. Now, with two words, it commanded the hidden voice reveal itself.

Her words echoed through the silence. Yet, the only sound that met her ears was a rustling that sounded suspiciously like the nervous shuffling of feet.

She took another step forward, refusing to retreat. Someone was definitely hiding in the shadows of the church graveyard, and it was her duty to oust them. She was, after all, employed by the church as the cleaning lady, which she was sure made her at least partially responsible for its well-being. If drifters were around, then the pastor would need to be notified. And until that could be done, she was more than able to take care of the problem herself.

Her hands curled tighter around the handle of her broom. The long wooden stick should be enough to subdue any drunk miner. The sliver of a moon wasn't enough to do more than bathe everything in a subtle glow. But her eyes caught movement and she focused, letting her vision separate a form from the surrounding darkness. She lifted her broom handle, her heart pounding in fear. Not giving her mind a chance to second guess her instincts, she swung, landing a blow right in the solid middle of the interloper.

A responding "oomph" was immediately followed by a wail.

"She got me! She got me!"

Disoriented, Leah only wanted the ear-piercing screeching to stop. She raised her broom for another blow, determined to prevent any further attack, verbal or otherwise.

With her weapon poised at its highest arc, ready to swoop down in a final blow, an arm shot up and grabbed the stick. Leah struggled, but the broom held tight within the fist holding it.

"Hold on there, Miss Leah!" a voice grumped as another hand perched on her shoulder. "No need to go swinging that pole around. No one needs to lay claim to a new grave tonight!"

"Mr. Tuft?" Leah stammered, recognizing the growl belonging to one of the church's parishioners. "What are you doing here?"

"We're just... um... holding a membership meeting."

A lamp was uncovered, revealing the faces of not one, but many of the regular church-goers. She also recognized the local liveryman, Frankie Smithers, still clutching his belly, having clearly been the victim of Leah's broom.

"Is the church locked?" Leah asked. "I didn't know there was a meeting scheduled for tonight." Leah looked around for the pastor. The church was rarely locked, but surely he had his keys.

However, the pastor's face was not to be found amongst the others, and by the furtive, guilty looks, she suddenly realized he hadn't been invited.

Into the awkward silence, another familiar voice spoke. "If you must know, we are holding a meeting regarding a gift for the pastor. We don't

wish to spoil the surprise, so we chose to meet here."
Winifred Beagle's tone dripped condescension.

"In the church cemetery?" Leah asked,
incredulous.

"Well, outside the church," Mrs. Beagle
clarified with a dignified tilt to her head "We didn't
exactly issue invitations for the venue."

Mr. Tuft, the owner of the local mercantile,
cleared his throat. "Seeing as how this is a...
surprise... for the good reverend, we sure would
appreciate you not mentioning our little discussion
tonight. That's why all the secrecy. We're trying to
agree on a really nice... present."

"Perhaps I could be of assistance," Leah
offered helpfully. Though the church congregation
was well-meaning, they were a rather colorful
assortment of characters, mostly a great deal older
than their pastor. Leah cringed to think what "gift"
they may be concocting. If she could give a little
direction to their intentions, perhaps they might save
the whole community some embarrassment. It was
widely agreed that they were very fortunate to have a
pastor in their small town, and for the good of a
mining town wishing to keep itself on the map, they
couldn't afford to lose one of their few earmarks to a
legitimate township.

Mrs. Beagle sniffed pompously. "Did you not
hear that this is a committee of *members*. Unless
you've aged since I saw you last Sunday, or found a
husband to marry you, you don't qualify, *Miss*
Barton. If I recall, you also have a job to do. We

don't want to disturb your cleaning. I'm fairly certain I witnessed a great deal of dirt being tracked into the sanctuary during Sunday service. Do I not hear it pleading for your attention?" The shadow of her hand flew in a shooing motion through the lantern's glow. "Now run along now. Your assistance is not required."

Leah felt the crush of the woman's words. Her attitude wasn't new. With her family background, Leah knew she was not acceptable to any "Christian" company. Oh, sure, they would follow the good book and assist her as a charity case. But never could she be included as an equal. Nevertheless, she couldn't stop herself from looking around the secretive group, looking for someone who would disagree with the foreboding Mrs Beagle, someone who would call her on her rude and demeaning treatment.

Yet no one would even meet Leah's gaze. Every face was down-turned or gazing into the distance, far off in the darkness beyond Leah and her cleaning supplies.

Leah felt the familiar burn of tears, but they didn't worry her. She was used to pushing the tears away. The only thing that did bother Leah was that it seemed that she should eventually stop feeling, that gradually, maybe she wouldn't feel the urge to cry so often.

But amazingly, that never happened. Though cruel comments were a daily occurrence, and the responsibilities and difficulties of her life were a constant drain, the same burning behind her eyes still assaulted her every time.

With an efficient nod, Leah gathered up her broom and other cleaning supplies and left the church members to conduct their graveyard tableau without her. She trudged up the steps of the church and pushed open the door. With a shaking hand, she lit the lamps around the sanctuary and readied to work, but her eyes were drawn to the darkened windows.

Resolutely, she began sweeping the sanctuary. She so wished she didn't have to work at night. But with three younger siblings to take care of, she really didn't have a choice. Her only time to work was either while two of the children were at school, or when they were all asleep. Since she already had other cleaning jobs, Reverend Moore had been kind enough to allow Leah to clean the church after she'd put the children to bed for the night. While convenient for helping to ensure they kept food on the table, it also meant the Leah often went without sleep.

Leah bent to retrieve a cleaning rag, feeling the weary muscles in her back protest. Once again, Leah bemoaned that she never seemed to adapt to her circumstances as she should. While she should stop needing to battle tears, she should also grow used to hard labor and little sleep. These weren't new circumstances.

There were two facts in her life that simply weren't ever going to change. One, her mother had died two years ago, leaving the full responsibility for a house and three children to fall on Leah's young shoulders. And two, her father was a drunk. And that fact had as much chance of changing as the first one. After watching Jim Barton's behavior for the past two years, Leah fully realized that her father had as much chance of not being a drunk as her mother had of being alive again.

Her eyes were once again drawn to the dark windows. She knew they were still out there, plotting a "gift" for their pastor. But what kind of present would require such elaborate planning and a clandestine meeting?

Quite likely, it was something their pastor would rather not have!

Leah liked Reverend Moore. He was a much better pastor than this community deserved. And Leah worried. What if the actions of a few eccentric members pushed him away?

Carefully setting down her broom, Leah crept over to the window. She had to know what they were planning. If she knew about their gift, then she could decide whether it was something the pastor should know about. She didn't trust them, and maybe, God had put her in this position to protect Reverend Moore.

Peering out the glass, Leah saw several bobbing lights and knew the meeting was still in session, but she couldn't tell much more than that. Though the church was fortunate to have real glass windows, paid for by the Beagles, of course, the windows themselves were very narrow and the glass had a cloudy hue. While they allowed light into the church, no one could actually see out.

Leah scurried to the door behind the pulpit. Cautiously, she opened it, hoping the seldom-used door wouldn't creak on its hinges. Opening it just wide enough, she slid her body through the gap.

Pausing, she listened. She could hear the voices from around the corner of the building. They were faint, but if she strained, she could barely make out the words. However, if she got just a little closer…

The church members were already concerned that she'd overhear their meeting. With a shallow little breath, Leah took a step, determined to do her best to oblige their fears.

Chapter 2

Leah's fingers gently lifted off the door handle, letting the door swing to balance in its slightly ajar position.

She stepped away, reaching her hand out to run along the rough wood side of the church.

With her first step, the door behind her creaked.

Leah froze.

"Did you hear that?" came the fierce whisper.

"Hear what?"

"Shhh!"

Leah held her breath. What would she do if they sent someone to investigate?

She felt the tick of the seconds as they matched her thudding heart.

Eventually, when Leah felt her lungs couldn't hold their air any longer, the whisper came again. "I guess it was nothing,"

Leah released her breath.

"Probably just that Barton girl stepping on a creaky board in the church," came another voice.

Leah crept forward, each gentle step silent in the soft dirt.

"We should have just sent her away. We can't trust her to not tell the reverend she saw us meeting." Leah recognized Winifred Beagle's voice.

"She'll be fine," a male voice said gruffly. Was that Mr. Tuft? "We didn't tell her anything important. But I wish you wouldn't have talked to her like that."

Mrs. Beagle sputtered. "Like what? Since we don't want the preacher to know, we should be careful who our audience is."

There was a pause. "Audience?" another voice asked. Leah was sure she recognized the drawl of Frankie Smithers. "You mean Miss Leah? She won't tell nobody. Maybe she could even help with our little project."

"Absolutely not," Mrs. Beagle objected.

Considering the woman's strident tone, Leah thought that, with a little effort, she may have been able to hear the conversation from inside the church, but she couldn't risk going back now. If she made any noise at all, they would come looking, and she would lose all chance of eavesdropping.

"We don't require help," Winifred Beagle continued, "especially from a non-member of questionable background and character."

Leah cringed. Respectable people never kept secret how they felt about her, Mrs. Beagle in particular. One wouldn't think that a California mining town would be so prejudicial, but that's the way the Beagles wanted it. This wasn't just any mining town. This was Secret. Sure, things could get wild with the number of prospectors that came through. But Secret actually had residents who called this their home. When Bill Beagle and his wife arrived here years ago, they came with a bank and the intention to make the community the hub of California gold country, leaving behind the wild ways of the Gold Rush to bring culture and permanence to a town that may have otherwise been abandoned with the shifting search for gold.

Now, with the transcontinental railroad winding through the Sierras and right through town, they knew they had their chance. If Secret was to fulfill the destiny the Beagles imagined, then some people, such as the daughter of the town drunk, were simply unacceptable.

She wished she could inch her head around the corner to watch, but she didn't dare. Just the simple movement might be enough to draw attention in the feeble moonlight. Instead, she would need to content herself with listening and using her imagination to paint the scene she heard.

"We've already agreed," Winifred said, her superior tone indicating that it was not a discussion worth her time. "I will fund the advertisement. With my connections, I can get it placed in prominent newspapers, and we are sure to receive high-quality candidates. Isn't that right, Mr. Beagle?"

Leah imagined Mr. Beagle giving his silent nod of approval. Whereas Mrs. Beagle was quite vocal on almost every subject, Mr. Beagle, though successful as the town's banker, was a man of few words and seemed to almost blend in with the large shadow cast by his wife.

"But you understand that you will not be making the selection yourself, Winifred," the male voice said suspiciously, clearly not completely convinced by the Beagles' reasoning.

Hearing the voice again, Leah was fairly certain this was Jarvis Tuft. Although the mercantile owner didn't have nearly the money of the Beagles, who owned just about everything besides the mercantile, Mr. Tuft was really the only man in town who was in a high enough social position to question Winifred Beagle.

"Remember?" Mr. Tuft continued. "We agreed that we shall convene as a committee again and review any applications together."

"Of course."

Leah scowled. Mrs. Beagle's tone was entirely too flippant and agreeable. Meaning she had some other plan. Meaning Leah didn't trust her, even a little.

Newspaper advertisements? Candidates? Reviewing applications? Exactly what kind of gift were they procuring for the pastor?

Mr. Tuft, apparently not overly suspicious of Mrs. Beagle's intentions, continued. "By the time we receive replies and decide on a candidate, we should have some time to all save money to contribute to her passage out west. With the trip taking several months, we should have plenty of time to tell the reverend and get prepared.

Her? Their gift was a *her*?

"Just think!" Frankie Smithers cackled. "A year from now, we'll have ourselves a real preacher's wife!"

Leah gasped. Clapping her hand against her own mouth, she tried to smother any further noise.

A bride! These people were ordering Reverend Moore a bride! Struggling with the shock, Leah still fought to pay attention to the appalling conversation.

"Oh, no!" Mrs. Beagle objected, clearly appalled. "That won't do at all! A year will be too late! Wouldn't you agree, Mr. Beagle?"

But without waiting for his response, Mrs. Beagle continued as if her husband had given his heartiest endorsement of her reasoning. "With the railroad and everyone coming west now that the war is over, we need to act now if we are going to be considered a legitimate, prosperous, family-oriented community attractive for people looking to settle. Having a young preacher in the pulpit with a wife and growing family is essential!"

"And how are we goin' to do that?" Frankie asked skeptically.

"Well, I suppose we don't have to go all the way back East to find a bride." Mr. Tuft mused thoughtfully. "If we get a woman from San Francisco, that would be a lot faster."

"That's right!" Frankie boomed enthusiastically. Then, as if suddenly unsure, he said, They do have women there right? And advertisements?"

"I think the female sort are still pretty few and far between in the city," Mr. Tuft admitted, "but it may be worth a try. We could send Frankie here down to fetch her. That would save a lot of time, and money too."

"Absolutely not!" Mrs. Beagle objected, highly offended. "If we want to make a good impression on future residents, we need a bride of quality. A woman of breeding who will be a credit to Reverend Moore and our community. The women in San Francisco are likely daughters of drunkards and miners, or maybe worse. Any decent woman will already be attached to a respectable suitor. You've spent time in San Francisco, Mr. Beagle. Don't you find my appraisal accurate?"

Frankie scoffed. "What's some highfalutin woman gonna do 'round here? The California gold fields ain't nothin' like it is back East, and there's no pretending it should be. No. Getting' a female from around these parts is a much better idea, and cheaper too. After we pick her, I could go fetch her and have her back in a matter of days."

Mr. Tuft spoke with certainty, "Winifred, you said we needed to do this quick. If that's what you really think, then San Francisco is the way to go."

Leah leaned against the church building for support. It didn't matter where they got a bride, she would still be a bride the reverend didn't order!

Leah kept hoping someone would speak up and say how ridiculous the idea actually was, but the other shadows clustered around the tombstones seemed content to silently listen to the three others discuss. The most they committed was an occasional grunt of agreement. To Leah's horror, it wasn't a discussion of if they were to get a bride, it was only when and how they would do so.

Mr. Tuft's words met the grunting assent of several shadows.

"Fine!" Mrs. Beagle snapped, blowing out an exasperated breath. "Fine! I'll put an advertisement in a San Francisco newspaper if it will make you happy. But since I am paying for this investment, I will also send telegrams to newspapers back East as well. You men are forgetting about the railroad. With its completion last year, letters from the applicants will arrive very quickly. Then, when we choose which one we want, I will send for her. With the railroad, she will get here in a fraction of the time it would take her to travel around the horn."

"Rail tickets will cost a pretty bag of gold," Frankie mused cautiously. "If we find a good woman in Frisco, I say we get her."

Mrs. Beagle answered firmly, "You are not going to be the one doing the paying. I will. Why do you care how much it costs?"

"This is not just your bride, Winifred." Mr. Tuft's words were stern. "She's *our* bride. She'll belong to all of Secret. If we are forming a church search committee to find her, then we all pitch in, just like you ladies do for the Ladies Aid Society."

"That's perfectly fine with me. Pardon me for trying to be kind." Mrs. Beagle's voice was almost petulant in its assumed offense. "I didn't want all of you to have to take food off your table in order to fund a bride. I planned to count the advertising and travel expenses as my donation for our community. After all, the town is the reason we are getting a reverend's wife. But if you can't see that I have the town's best interests at heart, then by all means, contribute some money. Missing a few meals never hurt anyone."

"It won't be a problem if we just fetch a woman from San Francisco," Frankie grumbled.

Mrs. Beagle snapped, "I already told you. There is not a decent woman to be found in all of California!"

"Well, given the example of womanhood we have right here, I might agree with that!" Franke retorted.

Leah's gasp was masked by Mrs. Beagle's own. But Leah's was quickly followed by a giggle that she attempted to smother. That Frankie Smithers didn't always seem like the brightest fellow, but every once in a while, he had his moments!

"Mr. Beagle," Mrs. Beagle bit out, enunciating each syllable with emphasis. "Do you hear the way they speak to me?"

But instead of Mr. Beagle, Mr. Tuft calmly spoke, his tone casual. "If the reverend hears your hollerin', he's sure to think the resurrection has happened and come to join us. Now, Winifred, you already agreed to put an advertisement in a San Francisco paper, along with the fancy Eastern ones."

The silent pause didn't include Mrs. Beagle's denial, which in this case was a good thing.

Mr. Tuft continued, "After Mrs. Beagle places ads in both places, we'll collect any letters we receive and decide together which woman should be our bride. If that woman happens to be from back East, Mrs. Beagle can cover the cost, if that's what she wants. But, if we vote, and our first choice is a woman from these parts, then Frankie can go load her up and haul her back."

"Fine," Mrs. Beagle said curtly. "I'll place the ads tomorrow. You'll soon find out San Francisco isn't worth our time."

"How soon will we get letters back?" Frankie asked. "When should we hold a meetin' to pick the bride?"

"We'll meet in a month," Mrs. Beagle replied confidently. "Hopefully, that should be sufficient time for responses. If we don't find one we like, we can always wait longer, but the sooner the better. Let's meet somewhere other than the graveyard, though."

"It is a bit gloomy," Frankie mused. "Though I can't help but think how many of our friends here would have somethin' to say about a preacher's wife. That Elmer over there sure did love a good society meetin'. Sure wish he hadn't gone and got himself shot."

Mrs. Beagle sniffed in distaste. "The graveyard being morbid, isn't what concerns me. It is the live, rather than the dead, audience who may be difficult to silence regarding our project."

Leah felt her face burn even though no one could see her. She knew that she was the "audience" Mrs. Beagle was referring to.

Frankie offered, "Mrs. Beagle, you let us know when you're ready with those letters, and we'll meet in the livery. Night is pretty quiet there, and Miss Leah don't do no cleanin' for me."

"I'm well aware that Miss Barton doesn't clean the livery," Mrs. Beagle snapped. "But you really mean that she doesn't do any cleaning for *me*. After all, I own the livery. You work for me, and the cleaning is your area of expertise, though judging from the smell, I have my doubts."

"Well, I do a might more than cleaning!" Frankie insisted, obviously offended. "But if you'd rather, I'm sure we could all meet at your house. I'll try not to haul any livery smell in with me."

"We're agreed then," Mr. Tuft said swiftly, before Mrs. Beagle could retort. "After Mrs. Beagle receives the letters of application, we will meet at the livery. You can expect the meeting to be in about a month, after Mrs. Beagle informs us that we are ready."

There was the sound of a voice clearing delicately.

"Yes, Mrs. Tuft. Do you have something to say?" Mrs. Beagle asked.

"I still don't like the idea of not talking to the preacher," she said hesitantly. "Are you sure he even wants a wife?"

"Of course he wants a wife!" Mrs. Beagle scoffed. "And it is our duty to provide one to him. The future of our town depends on it."

Mrs. Tuft was a soft-spoken woman. Her quiet, gentle personality didn't seem to belong in a mining town. Leah had heard that Mr. Tuft's mercantile had been a compromise. When Jarvis Tuft had wanted to come out west to seek his fortune, Ellen Tuft had objected. She was obviously from a more genteel background, while Jarvis, being more rough around the edges, was eager for adventure beyond city life.

Finally, her inheritance had gone to investing in the mercantile, which Ellen had determined much preferable to actual mining. Though the couple had been quite successful in their venture over the years, Ellen was still quite reserved, rarely becoming involved in anything to do with the community. The fact that she even mentioned an objection now was likely unprecedented.

"But what if he wants to choose his own from the women around here?" she ventured softly.

Her words were met with shocked silence. It was unheard of that Mrs. Tuft raise any objection, let alone a persistent two!

"What women are you talking about?" Mrs. Beagle finally managed, her voice barely concealing scorn. "Last I heard, the female population of Secret numbers around five. If we want our pastor to stay and put down roots in our town, then we need to provide him with a wife with whom to start a family."

"Now, I think there be a mite few more than five lady folk around here," Frankie mused. "There's Miss Ameberly and Miss Rosalyn and Madame—"

"My point exactly!" Mrs. Beagle laughed. "I don't think Reverend Moore would care to choose his bride from the scarlet ladies of Secret!"

Leah still thought Mrs. Beagle's point was exaggerated. There were more than five acceptable women in Secret. If Leah was to guess, she thought that Mrs. Tuft's background was of a higher pedigree than Mrs. Beagle, though it is unlikely Mrs. Beagle would ever concede such a point. However, just because those two women were the most prominent in terms of social standing, that didn't mean there weren't others who would be acceptable to be a pastor's wife. The saloon girls were out of the question, of course, but that didn't mean there weren't widows, or daughters of miners, or young women whose background may not be the most desirable but who were hardworking, God-fearing women.

"If we don't give him a good reason to stay, he will leave," Mrs. Beagle said sternly. "A young clergyman as accomplished as Jeremiah Moore doesn't stay in a town like Secret unless he puts down roots."

"We sure do want him to stay," Frankie admitted, somewhat uneasily. "He's mighty entertainin' on a Sunday mornin'. Shoot, if we get a bride and he doesn't want her, I'll take her."

"If we are careful in our selection, I'm sure Reverend Moore will be pleased," Mr. Tuft said thoughtfully. "We don't really have anything to lose. Frankie is right in that, if the worst happens and the pastor doesn't want his bride, there will be many others willing to fill his shoes and get a good woman as a wife."

"If I'm the one haulin' her back from the city, then I get first claim after the preacher." Frankie insisted. "I can tell you right now, ain't no one goin' be claim jumpin' me for a woman!"

Leah left the two men to argue over the bride rights and slunk back along the side of the church to the door. She knew she'd better be busy inside cleaning in case Mrs. Beagle came in to check on her before she left for home.

The door made only the slightest of creaks as she opened it wide enough to slip her body back through. She picked up her broom and quickly went to work sweeping.

Leah felt sick to her stomach and almost wished she hadn't eavesdropped on the meeting.

This was a bad situation, for sure. The church members had appointed themselves as a committee to order Reverend Moore a wife, whether he wanted one or not.

And Leah was certain he would not. That meant that somebody needed to inform the reverend before his church placed their bridal order.

Feeling even more ill, Leah stopped her furious sweeping and sank to the wood-planked floor with the broom held loosely in her lap.

There was only one somebody who could warn Reverend Moore of his impending nuptials. And, unfortunately, that somebody was Leah Barton.

Chapter 3

"Reverend Moore!"

Mr. Tuft's greeting sent Leah's heart to pounding before the bell over the door stopped its welcoming jingle.

Reverend Moore had arrived, exactly as Leah knew he would. He checked the mail at the same time every day. But this time was different. Instead of trying to stay out of the way and not draw attention to herself, Leah knew she needed to speak with him about his congregation's plans for mutiny. If they were ordering Reverend Moore a bride, Leah thought it right that the groom should know about it!

Leah bit her lip anxiously, pausing in her sweeping to watch the smiling pastor greet the others in the mercantile. He really was a nice, friendly sort. Though Leah wouldn't admit it, she liked to watch him. He was so tall and lean that he looked rather scrawny compared to some of the rough miners, but Leah had seen him help around town and knew he could chop and carry firewood just as well as anyone.

It was a mystery to Leah as to why he'd chosen this town. In every way Leah could tell, he was too good for it: too handsome, too young, too educated, too well-mannered, and too smart. Yet, here he was, greeting and conversing with all of the miners and rough characters in Secret as if they were the cream of society.

He was well-liked by all, and with his daily trips to the mercantile, he was able to keep up on the people and goings-on. If he wanted to know about those who needed help or prayer, then the Tuft's Mercantile was the place to be.

In Secret, the mercantile also served as the post office and general hub of the community, a fact that Mrs. Beagle didn't seem to appreciate. According to snippets of conversation Leah had overheard, Mrs. Beagle's plans for the community included a real post office as well as a fancy hotel, all owned by the Beagles, of course.

Apparently, the first step in that plan to turn Secret into the town jewel of the Sierras, was to get a preacher's wife.

And that first step was the one Leah needed to intercept.

The problem was that it wouldn't be proper for Leah to meet with the pastor privately. Not that her reputation was a huge risk; her background already made others doubt her character. But she would never want to cast any question on the good pastor. It also wasn't a conversation she wanted to have publicly. If the congregation knew she had eavesdropped and spoiled their secret, then she would be ridiculed and even more of an outcast. She also didn't want to cause the reverend any undue embarrassment, though Leah didn't know how unavoidable that was when the daughter of the town drunk had to break the news that your congregation was conspiring to procure you a wife.

So the task at hand was to tell Reverend Moore in a public place, but in a discreet way. And accomplish it before Mrs. Beagle came in to place the telegrams!

Leah watched as Reverend Moore went to the counter to retrieve his mail. Quietly, she tiptoed down the aisle and positioned herself so that he would have to pass by her as he left. Keeping watch out of the corner of her eye, she pretended to be busy dusting. She removed each item from the shelf, swiping beneath it with a rag before replacing it. Hopefully no one would notice that there wasn't a speck of dust on the shelf. Leah had already cleaned it once today.

The Tufts were kind enough to employ her cleaning services a few days a week. With the church and the mercantile, she was able to keep food on the table for her little siblings. But the cleaning usually only took her a couple of hours. Since she began right after the older children went to school, this mid-morning time was pushing the limits of her schedule. She didn't want to take advantage of the Tuft's good will and be seen as dawdling.

Unfortunately, Reverend Moore was taking his time talking with Mr. Tuft.

If Leah was any less nervous, she could have actually paid attention to their conversation, but as it was, she was too busy mentally rehearsing what she would say.

Finishing with the assortment of ribbons, Leah moved on to rearranging the bolts of fabric. Feeling slightly guilty, she purposely moved the pretty white calico to the bottom of the pile. She didn't realistically think there was any way she would ever be able to hide enough money from her father so that she could buy the material for a dress, and white was terribly frivolous and impractical. But that lofty dream still made her hope the material wouldn't be noticed by other customers if it was on the bottom of the stack.

As soon as he turns around, ask if you can have a minute of his time, she coached herself. *Maybe I start with, "Good Morning." Or maybe—*

He smiled goodbye to Mr. Tuft and turned.

Now was her chance!

"Reverend Moore," she began breathlessly. "May I—"

"Miss Barton, I must have a word with you!"

Leah jumped at the sharp voice. Turning, she found Mr. Schantz, the schoolmaster, at her elbow.

And at his elbow was Leah's six-year-old brother, Curtis.

"Miss Barton, I am here to remind you that it is unacceptable for ill children to be sent to school. I believe we have already discussed this. It exposes all of the other students, and me. Regardless of your circumstances, it is your responsibility to care for your sick brother, not mine!"

Leah sidled an embarrassed glance in the direction of Reverend Moore. Unfortunately, his wary gaze was taking in every word spoken by the schoolmaster.

Leah swallowed, her throat dry. "Is Curtis ill, Mr. Schantz?"

"Of course he is! He has a fever and expelled all over his school desk! The other children are outside for their lunch while I had to search all of Secret to find you! Now I have to go clean up his mess! Needless to say, I hold you responsible!"

Leah felt a burning starting at her neck and quickly spreading up her face. Here she was wanting to appear respectable and conscientious in front of the reverend! Now she struggled to hold her head up under Mr. Schantz's lecture.

What would Reverend Moore think of her now?

Trying to keep her quiet tone dignified, Leah spoke, "Mr. Schantz, I apologize, but Curtis was fine this morning when I sent him to school. I would never send him if I knew he was ill. I will come to the school and clean up the mess right away. But first let me get Curtis home and in bed and pick up

Hazel from Mrs. Pope. She could only watch my sister until noon."

"Mrs. Pope is the one who told me where to find you. And she said to tell you to hurry as her rheumatism is acting up something fierce." Mr. Schantz paused, the scowl on his face deepening. "I don't like it, but the students and I will take our lessons outside until you are able to come clean up after your brother."

"Thank you, Mr. Schantz," Leah said with relief.

Mr. Schantz was not a pleasant man to deal with in even the happiest of circumstances. He was a rough man, not matching the typical schoolmaster type. Apparently gold fever could affect anyone, even the highly educated. And Mr. Schantz had come out west to make his fortune in the gold mines, just like everyone else.

Unfortunately, he had failed miserably and lost what little money he had to begin with. Because of his education, the Beagles had offered him the position of schoolmaster. Left with no other options, he had accepted and spent the time since then making the students and everyone in the community regret that placement. From what Leah could tell, he was an adequate instructor, but his gruff, angry attitude made him quite unpopular.

Though Leah didn't relish the thought of being on his bad side, she didn't think he had a good side, so she had to manage the best she could. His acceptance of her offer to clean up the mess didn't seem like much, but Leah would take the small victory, especially if it meant ending his lecture.

Mr. Schantz looked momentarily disturbed, as if troubled that he lacked reason to further his complaint.

Thinking their interview over, Leah nodded to the pastor, though she didn't meet his gaze, and moved to pass Mr. Schantz, Curtis's hand firmly tucked in hers.

But the schoolmaster didn't move to let her by.

Looking up in confusion, Leah watched his mouth narrow into a stern pout, another idea forming and adding fuel for his ready anger. Apparently cleaning up Curtis's mess wasn't deemed enough punishment.

Leah braced herself for the next onslaught.

"When you arrive at the school, your other brother, Johnny, will also be waiting for you. You may take him home as well." Mr. Schantz nodded firmly, his mind made up as if this had been his plan all along.

"Is he sick as well?" Leah asked confusedly.

"No, Miss Barton, Johnny Barton is *suspended.*"

Leah swallowed. Johnny was not an easy child, but he had never been suspended before. In general, the schoolmaster took care of his own discipline.

Leah didn't know what to say. Was Mr. Schantz doing this just because he was angry at them about Curtis being ill?

"Pardon me," a new voice said. "I couldn't help but overhear. Mr. Schantz, I'm sure Miss Barton would find it helpful to know her brother's infraction."

With relief, Leah shot Reverend Moore a look of appreciation. "Yes, I would."

Mr. Schantz pursed his lips. "He put a mouse in my desk drawer."

"Again?" Leah gasped, horrified. "But he promised me last year that he would never put a dead mouse in your desk again. Are you sure it was him?"

If Mr. Schantz was right, then Johnny well-deserved to be suspended! After the incident last year, Leah felt that she'd finally gotten through to him, and extracted a promise that it would never happen again. Now she was sorely disappointed in her 8-year-old brother!

"I am positive," the schoolmaster said, clearly enunciating each word. "With Curtis being sick today, Johnny is the only one in the class who would partake in such behavior. He is suspended for the day. And if I ever find a mouse of any kind in my desk again, he will be expelled! Unless that boy has a good encounter with Almighty God, he'll follow directly in his father's footsteps. Mark my words, Miss Barton, Bad Bart will have an heir!"

Leah fought to control the instant tears that sprang to her eyes at the man's harsh words. She was doing the best she could to raise her siblings, and yet Mr. Schantz just hit on her greatest fear.

Before she could find the first syllable of a proper apology, Reverend Moore's voice took over, "Mr. Schantz, I don't think—"

"Miss Leah! I'm glad I caught you before you left for the day!" Frankie Smithers bustled up, whipping off his hat to reveal his round, rosy face. Not seeming to notice the dour Mr. Schantz, or a visibly perturbed reverend, Frankie eagerly gave his report. "I just thought you'd like to know that I spotted Johnny making off with a wheelbarrow full of manure. Now I don't know what a boy would need with manure this time of year. Would you be working on your garden, Miss Leah? Anyways, I thought you might be on the lookout for it. Don't think I'd be needin' any stolen manure back, though," he chuckled good-naturedly. "He's more'n welcome to keep it. Just thought you should know."

"Good heavens!" Mr. Schantz exclaimed. "A wheelbarrow full of manure?"

Without waiting for an answer, Mr. Schantz turned and sprinted down the aisle and out the door of the mercantile.

Leah shut her eyes, praying for strength. Opening them, she nodded to Frankie, "Thank you for letting me know, Mr. Smithers. I'm not sure why Johnny took the manure, but I will certainly find out."

"Aw, Miss Leah, I done told you before to just call me Frankie, like everyone else. You let me know if you want me to come teach that Johnny a good lesson for you."

Leah forced a smile and turned to the counter, seeing Mr. Tuft enter from the back. He apparently hadn't been around to witness Leah's audience with Mr. Schantz. "Mr. Tuft," she called quietly. "I am done for the day. Curtis here is ill and I have some other matters to attend to."

Mr. Tuft nodded. "It looks as if you already cleaned everything, Miss Leah. We'll see you tomorrow."

With her brother's hand in hers, she tucked her cleaning supplies under her other arm, and started for the door. "Thank you for your assistance, Reverend Moore," she said quietly, not daring to meet his gaze.

"Miss Barton!" Reverend Moore called, stopping her with a gentle hand to her elbow. "Is there anything I can do to help? I believe you were wanting to speak with me before Mr. Schantz arrived?"

Leah looked down at the hand lightly touching her elbow, feeling confused that such a feather-light pressure could make her feel so dizzy. She looked back up, catching Reverend Moore's steel-gray eyes. She held them briefly, only to falter when she realized who was standing behind him at the counter.

Mrs. Beagle, having entered in the drama from Mr. Schantz's departure, was quietly giving instructions for the telegrams.

It was too late.

"Umm..." she said, trying to think of a graceful exit from the conversation that wouldn't include outright lying.

She felt a tug on the skirt of her dress. Looking down, she saw brown hair and two pale blue eyes, so much like her own, looking stark in a white, miserable little face. She needed to get Curtis home to rest.

"How is Miss Jolly?" she blurted, hoping her random question would have a short answer "I heard you called on her yesterday evening."

Reverend Moore nodded seriously. "She is not faring well, I'm afraid. The doctor is arriving for his regular circuit through town this afternoon. I will take him to call on her then."

"I will be sure to check on her when I am able," Leah offered. "She is so kind to watch Hazel for me on most days. Please let me know if there is anything I can do for her."

"Pray," the pastor said with a sad smile.

"Of course," Leah answered.

"And you look as if you might need some prayer yourself, young man," he said turning to Curtis with a smile.

The boy nodded weakly.

Holding the boy's hand, Leah gently pulled him to the door, which Reverend Moore held open for her.

"Miss Barton, why don't I escort young Mr. Curtis home while you go attend to things at the schoolhouse. I will stay with him until you arrive."

Leah hesitated. "I'm sure I can manage," she said. "You must be busy, and I don't want you to get sick from Curtis."

"Nonsense," the pastor said, easily brushing off her objections. "Part of my job is helping the sick. I insist. I'm sure Mr. Schantz will appreciate your prompt attention."

"Thank you," Leah said, reluctantly letting Reverend Moore take Curtis's small hand from hers. "My father might be home... sleeping," she said self-consciously. She wasn't sure how to delicately say that her father might still be hung over from drinking last night and not really fit for a pastoral visit. Leah never knew what state her father would be in when she arrived home, but she couldn't really condense the mess that was her family into a short phrase palatable for a reverend.

Reverend Moore's warm gaze met hers, and she saw a light of understanding flash. He nodded. "Don't worry, Miss Barton. We will be fine until you arrive home."

Leah wasn't used to having anyone even offer to help her, so this situation felt strange. However, not given another option, she hurried to the schoolhouse while the pastor slowly escorted Curtis down the boardwalk in the opposite direction.

Ignoring Mr. Schantz and the other students outside the small one-room building, she entered and made quick work of the mess. Her urge to hurry was intensified by the thought of the pastor in her house... seeing the mess left by the children... caring for her brother... encountering her pa. After she was done, she put away the school's cleaning supplies back into the storage closet at the rear of the classroom, gathered the other supplies that belonged to her, and marched outside. Not bothering to make an announcement or even spare another word to Mr. Schantz, she descended the steps to where Johnny was sulking while seated on the bottom plank.

Pulling him to his feet, Leah gripped his elbow tightly, and began urging him along toward home. She didn't glare at him or chide him. Leah hated that she would need to think of some parental consequences for the boy, and at the moment, she just wasn't up for it. It wasn't right that an older sister would need to take on that responsibility, but she was the only one who would.

For right now, she just let her anger exude through her sharp movements and brisk walk. Johnny hurried to keep up. Out of the corner of her eye, she saw him shooting nervous glances at her every few steps. He knew he was in trouble, and her silence was probably bothering him more than any lecture.

Not a word did she speak to him when they stopped to pick up her four-year-old sister, Hazel, from Mrs. Pope's house. Not a word did she speak to him as she marched down the street of Secret, carrying Hazel because she was in too big of a hurry to let the girl's little legs determine the schedule.

Ignoring the frequent glances Johnny sent her way, her own feet hurried to the small shack on the edge of town. As her eyes caught sight of it, she thought with embarrassment about what it looked like to others, specifically Reverend Moore.

It was amazing that in a place as beautiful as the Sierra Mountains, that such an eyesore of a home existed. It would be different if it was in the midst of some tall pine trees where you couldn't really see it too well. But instead, it was plopped down in a cleared section with a few other of the same sort of buildings scattered around. They looked almost like outhouses, but a bit bigger.

Theirs had no windows and boasted only two rooms. Overall, it looked as if someone decided to build a house with no prior planning. At night. After he'd just spent the entire evening at the saloon.

And truthfully, it may have happened that way. Two years ago, shortly after her mother's death, Leah's father had come home to their little house on their claim, packed up their things, and moved them here. From what Leah later heard from the rumors around town, he had lost their claim and house in a bet.

Though the roof leaked, and the entire thing looked like it may fall over with one breath from the big, bad wolf, the worst part of the situation was that they didn't even own the place. The Beagles did. Every month, Leah had to scrape together enough money to pay for their rent. The property where the house sat was a large tract of land where, for a monthly fee, the Beagles let tenants build their own shelter, or even pitch a tent in the summer. Leah didn't know if her father threw their "shelter" together two years ago, or if it was here already. But either way, it was a sad place to be.

And Leah hated to think of the pity she knew she would read in Reverend Moore's eyes after he'd seen how they lived.

"I guess you're mad," Johnny said, bringing Leah back to the boy beside her. They were almost home, and it seemed like Johnny couldn't handle the silent treatment any longer.

Leah needed no more invitation. Turning on him, she put her hands on her hips, ready to deliver a well-deserved lecture that would make her ma proud. "Yes, Johnny, I'm mad. You told me you wouldn't put a mouse in Mr. Schantz desk again. You *promised*. It is very hurtful and disappointing that you broke that promise!"

"But, Leah, I didn't break my promise!" Johnny said adamantly.

His words would have made Leah even more angry except the tears welling up in his eight-year-old eyes gave her pause. "Yes, you did, Johnny," she insisted, though not roughly. "You said you wouldn't do it, and you did. That's breaking your promise."

"I did not!" His hands perched on his hips, matching her position. "I promised that I wouldn't put a dead mouse in Mr. Schantz's desk again, and I didn't!"

Leah rolled her eyes. "Then what exactly did you put in Mr. Schantz's desk, Johnny?"

The boy sniffled, as if his feelings were a bit bruised by her unfair treatment of him. "I don't know what that teacher told you, but that mouse was definitely alive when I put him in there!"

Realizing her current conversation was completely hopeless, Leah threw up her hands in exasperation and marched toward the house. She could only hope that any conversation she found inside would be considerably less aggravating.

Chapter 4

Her stomach wrenched at the sight that met her when she walked through the door. Curtis was bent over a bucket vomiting while Reverend Moore sat beside him with a hand to his back in comfort.

"Oh, Reverend Moore, let me do that!" Leah exclaimed, hurrying over to take his place. He moved aside, but still hovered close. When Curtis was done, Leah wiped his brow and face with a wet rag, then helped him to his bed in the corner. Even though Leah kept a firm hold of his arm and tried to support his weight, he stumbled weakly, and Leah barely managed to catch him before he toppled to the floor.

Without a word, Reverend Moore scooped Curtis up in his arms, carried him over to his pine bough mattress, and laid him down gently.

"Thank you," Leah whispered as she smoothed Curtis's hair back and placed another bucket beside him. Leah took the first bucket outside and made quick work of emptying and cleaning it before returning inside. "Don't feel like you have to stay, Reverend Moore. I know you have other duties to attend. I really appreciate your help."

"Do you think he needs a doctor?" the pastor asked, concerned. "I could bring Doc Morgan over here after he sees Miss Jolly this afternoon."

"No, I don't think that will be necessary," Leah said quickly. "I'm sure he'll feel better tomorrow." What she didn't say was that there was no way she could afford a doctor, even if it was necessary.

"I don't really have any obligations until fetching the doctor later this afternoon," Reverend Moore said. "If there is anything I can do, I'd like to help you out in some way. I know it can't be easy providing for and managing your three siblings, especially with one of them ill. Is there anything you need repaired around the house?"

Leah almost laughed as the pastor looked around, speculating on possible projects. Did the entire house count as a project? It would be easier to list the things that didn't need repaired.

Leah tried to think of something she could ask him to do that wouldn't be too embarrassing to her sense of pride and too time-consuming for his generous offer. Leah didn't want to take advantage of him, but she also didn't want to offend him by rejecting his help. He really was so nice.

Trying to match the good pastor with an appropriate project, Leah looked at him, really looked at him.

Leah knew he had been in the war, but he was still young, maybe at most ten years older than Leah's nineteen years. Her gaze skimmed the dark brown frame of his neatly-combed brown hair, then traced his clean-shaven face, looking for any scars or remnants from his time in the war. But she found nothing, until she got to his eyes. The steel gray had depth and a hint of a shadow, revealing a maturity that was likely achieved through witnessing things no person should ever see.

He wasn't like the other men around the California mountains. But it wasn't just the lack of scraggly beard, unkempt clothes, and foul odor. To Leah, most of the miners had a desperate, crazed look in their eyes. It was almost animalistic, as if they were hungry predators hunting for the last piece of meat before another animal took it away. Gold did strange things to people, and Leah had come to recognize the look of gold fever in a man's eye. But Reverend Moore was different. Though his eyes definitely held the specter of grief, they also carried a peace, as if he had already found what other men were spending their lifetimes searching for.

Leah suddenly realized that while she was studying the pastor, he was studying her. She self-consciously looked away and wondered if she should go check on Johnny and Hazel outside. Or maybe her father. Should she check on him?

Her gaze nervously drifted toward the closed door. Was he even home? Had Reverend Moore encountered him?

As if her questions had been verbalized, Reverend Moor answered, "He stuck his head out before you arrived. He said something, but I didn't understand. Then he shut the door again."

Her gaze caught on his one more time. The look he gave her held such understanding and compassion that she felt tears burn the back of her eyes.

Reverend Moore was a good man. He deserved better than to have his ragtag congregation force a bride of their choice on him. Even if Mrs. Beagle had already placed the ad, the pastor deserved to know. Maybe there was still time.

Leah took a deep breath. "Could I get you some lunch, Reverend? I need to feed the children, and truthfully, rather than a project, there is something I'd like to discuss with you."

The pastor smiled. "I'd like that very much."

Leah checked on Curtis and found him sleeping, which she was very thankful for. Hopefully his body would get the rest it needed, and he wouldn't spoil the pastor's appetite with another retching episode.

While Leah heated a pot of beans on the stove, Reverend Moore found a chair with a broken leg and began fixing it.

Leah wished she had better fare to offer the pastor, but beans and homemade bread were all she had. She was occasionally able to purchase some meat, or sometimes one of the church members was kind enough to bring her some of the game from a hunting expedition, but most of the time, they just got by. Most likely, the beans and bread would also be the dinner meal as well.

Leah had considered taking her father's gun and learning to hunt, but when she had broached the subject with him, he had become angry and refused. Saying that it was his responsibility to provide, he had marched out of the house with his gun, only to return drunk hours later, with no meat.

Leah knew the pastor likely took most of his meals at the restaurant, along with the majority of other men in the area. She knew her food couldn't compare with his usual fare, but she pushed back the embarrassment and loaded a plate with a generous serving of beans and a thick slice of bread.

"Why don't we eat outside?" she suggested. "While we talk, I can watch the children and not worry about disturbing Curtis."

"That would be nice," Reverend Moore said agreeably, helping to carry out plates of food for Johnny and Hazel.

Leah located some wooden crates that they could use as chairs and the good pastor was kind enough not to remark on the fact that they were all whiskey crates.

The children were done and off to play before Leah sat down and took five bites of food. Leah had wanted to ask Johnny about the wheelbarrow full of manure, but seeing him busily working on some boy project involving raking a bunch of the leaves and debris from around the house, she decided to wait to question him until after Reverend Moore left. For right now, with the crates positioned on a narrow strip of wood that attempted to be the house's front porch, she at least had a good view of any further mischief Johnny caused as Hazel followed him around.

Leah ate slowly, trying to figure out a way to bring up the subject of the pastor's surprise wife. But every time she thought she just needed to come and say it outright, doubts crept in. Maybe she was wrong about all of this. Maybe he would actually appreciate a mail order bride.

"Why did you come to Secret, Reverend Moore?" Leah finally asked quietly.

"Well, the short answer is that I saw an advertisement," he said with a smile. "Mrs. Beagle posted an advertisement for a pastor for the community. I saw the ad and answered it."

"Mrs. Beagle does seem to like her advertisements..." Leah took a deep breath, preparing to launch the bride story.

"I somehow doubt you're interested in the short answer, though," Reverend Moore mused. "I've seen the way you watch people, Miss Barton. You don't say much, but you're curious and interested. I have a feeling you're not really a short answer person."

"Is that wrong?" Leah asked, a little unnerved that he had so accurately observed her. He had been here six months now, but this was the first time she had held a conversation with him. With her background and circumstances, it hadn't seemed proper for her to be friendly with the pastor. She usually just attended church and did her work with her head down, trying not to be noticed. Obviously, she hadn't quite succeeded. Reverend Moore had indeed been watching.

"No, not at all. You're likely a very good observer, which can give you insight on how to talk to and help people. Now, if you were to spread secrets and gossip about your observations, that would be different. But you don't."

Leah swallowed. Would he consider it gossip for her to tell him what she'd overheard about the congregation's surprise?

Looking her straight, earnestly in the eyes, he continued, "I'll make you a deal, Miss Barton. I will tell you my full story on two conditions. One, that you stop calling me Reverend Moore. I know it's proper, but we're in the Wild West. At least when the Beagles aren't around, can you please call me by my given name, Jeremiah?"

Leah hesitantly nodded. "And reason number two?"

"I know you want to talk to me about something. This is the second time today that you've tried. If I tell you my story, you must agree to tell me what's bothering you."

Leah's mouth went dry. Jeremiah Moore was too discerning, too nice, and entirely too handsome for Leah's comfort.

But she nodded again. "Why did you come to Secret... Jeremiah?"

Jeremiah leaned back and looked out toward the yard area dotted with Leah's little flock of chickens and children busy on their project, but he seemed to be looking past them. "I was in the war. When I enlisted in the Union army, I wanted to be a chaplain. But that didn't last. Battle after battle took good men from both sides, with no one to replace them. It wasn't long before I was wielding a gun just like all the others. I was a soldier, and I accepted that, choosing ministry in between gunshots. I was one of the few who came out of the war intact, and I still wanted to be a minister. I got some education at a university, but it took me a few years of working my way through. After I graduated, I felt God wanted me out West. My family always thought I should pastor the large church in the town where I grew up, but I didn't want that. I wanted to be out here on the frontier, where the need for God is raw and church is less tied to tradition. So I guess I kind of ran away."

"What do you mean?" Leah asked, finding it difficult to imagine the strong man before her running away from anything.

"I did the opposite of what my parents wanted. To them, I was inconsiderate and a disappointment, but after seeing all of the towns, fields, and people of the East through the filter of war, it was all repugnant to me. I longed to get away. I felt such a strong call that I came across the country, with no real destination. When I arrived in San Francisco, I wandered around, not really knowing what to do or how to do it. I saw a newspaper tumbling down the street in the breeze. I grabbed it, intending to throw the piece of trash away. The strange thing was that it was an Eastern paper, not even printed in San Francisco. Then, I glanced across the advertisements and stumbled on one searching for a pastor in Secret, California. Since it was an older newspaper, I sent a telegram asking if the position was still open. When I found out it was, I sent my qualifications and a letter to the Beagles. Three weeks later was my first Sunday preaching at the church."

"I'm sure the Beagles thought it very fortunate to find a pastor already in California that was so qualified," Leah commented, marveling at the story that brought him to their community. "All of Secret seems to like you. They want you to stay, but I think they're worried you'll get a better offer from a bigger town and leave."

There! She'd brought up the subject. Sort of.

"No one can know for sure where God will call them in the future. But I'm not looking to leave Secret. I like it here. I fully believe that God is the one who made me pick up that newspaper and showed me the ad. I look at it as a wonderful example of God's providence. I'm where God wants me."

Leah opened her mouth to reply, but suddenly she lost the words

If Jeremiah thought Mrs. Beagle's advertisement brought him here because of God's providence, maybe he'd see an ad for a bride in the same light!

Jeremiah looked at her expectantly, waiting for her to say something.

Now was her chance.

"Do you… want some cake?" she finished pathetically.

"Sure," he responded, looking a little startled at her random subject change.

Seeing that Johnny was busy spreading leaves and weeds over the general area of his project and Hazel was skipping around him collecting summer's last wildflowers, Leah hurriedly bustled back into the house, eager to have a moment to rein in her panic and collect her stampeding thoughts.

What should she do? Working to calm herself, she tried to pray while she cut a generous piece of the berry cake she had made yesterday.

Maybe Jeremiah would actually appreciate the congregation's efforts. He said he liked it here. If God had used an advertisement to bring Jeremiah to Secret, who was to say that He wouldn't use an advertisement to bring Jeremiah a wife? And who was Leah to interfere with something that may be God's will?

But it still just didn't seem right.

Leah walked back outside with still no clear answer as to what she needed to do. She handed him the cake and nervously sat back down on her whiskey box.

Jeremiah wasted no time in taking a large bite of the cake. As soon as he put it in his mouth, he paused, a strange look on his face.

"Is something wrong with the cake?" Leah asked worriedly. "I just made it yesterday!"

Jeremiah shook his head. "On the contrary, it's delicious. It just reminds me of a similar cake I had with Miss Jolly. You said you made it yesterday?"

"Yes," Leah said cautiously. "The children picked some berries. They always love berry cake."

"Miss Jolly said someone left her the cake outside her door yesterday." He turned speculative eyes her direction. "It tasted remarkably like this one."

Leah felt a blush and hurried to respond. "It's my mother's recipe. It may be a common one around here."

Jeremiah's eyebrows raised, and his mouth quirked, as if he was trying to control his laugher. "Yes, because there are so many women in Secret… who bake cakes."

Leah looked at the children, at the chickens, at the trees—anywhere but at Jeremiah.

But the pastor still studied her with a knowing gaze. "Miss Jolly says she often has things left at her door—berries, bread, cakes, flowers. It lifts her spirits to see what gifts are left for her and to know someone thinks of her."

"Miss Jolly is such a nice person," Leah said conversationally. "She's always helping others. She was my mother's closest friend before she passed. When Miss Jolly is well, she takes care of Hazel for me while I clean. She never asks for anything in return. I would imagine that anyone who knows Miss Jolly loves and appreciates her. Some of those people might try to show their thanks in whatever little way they are able, especially since she hasn't been well and is unable to do a lot of baking."

"That makes sense," Jeremiah nodded. "But I think it takes a special, thoughtful person to do that for her. And to do it anonymously is even more admirable."

Leah shrugged. " 'Let not thy left hand know what thy right hand doeth…' "

If possible, the admiration in Jeremiah's eyes glowed even more brightly. "Matthew 6:3."

Leah nodded. "If Miss Jolly's benefactor doesn't wish to be identified, it seems like a good secret to keep. He or she isn't looking for recognition from others. Some secrets are worth keeping."

And some secrets aren't worth keeping.

She didn't want to be the one to have to tell Jeremiah about his congregation's secret bride. But there was no spiritual reward in letting them order a bride without his consent.

Jeremiah stood from his crate and stretched. Taking a few paces toward the children, his foot found the step from the porch to the ground. But the instant his weight hit the loose board, it bucked him awkwardly off the porch. Catching himself before he fell, he turned around and flashed a grin at Leah. "I'd better fix that before someone with a little less grace than me encounters that step."

At his request, Leah found him a can of nails and a hammer. By the time, he bent his tall frame down to secure the step, Leah was barely controlling her emotion. He could have been upset that the step was loose in the first place. He could have yelled and stomped around, then left in a huff as her father was want to do. He could have just left the step alone for her to deal with.

But no, that wasn't the kind of man he was.

Which Leah took to mean that he *was* the kind of man who deserved to be told the truth.

With determination, she lifted her face to look at him directly.

But with his gaze focused on the nail in his hand, he spoke idly, before she could get the words out.

"Miss Barton, why aren't you married?"

Leah blinked in surprise, and all the words she had gathered to say suddenly retreated.

Then, as if realizing what he'd just said, he hesitated, then hurried to clarify. "I mean, there aren't many women around here, especially ones who are God-fearing and can bake delicious cakes. You must get ten marriage proposals a week."

"Please, call me Leah. If you are Jeremiah, I am Leah." Her smile turned sad. "I'm not exactly marriageable material in this town. You haven't been here long, so I'm sure you aren't aware of my family's history. Though this is a frontier, mining community, people are still very opinionated. I am not ever considered as an option for any gentleman because of my father's habits at the local saloon. And for the miners, I'm not an attractive catch because I come with three children in the package deal. My siblings are my responsibility. I could never leave them for a home of my own, and any decent man would object to a ready-made family and a wife with a less than ideal reputation. I'm not worth it."

"Leah, you would be worth that and much more to the right kind of man," Jeremiah quietly insisted.

Leah shook her head. "Don't feel bad for me, Jeremiah. Since my mother passed, I've never really considered marriage an option for me, so I don't feel the sting of being deprived. I haven't met a miner I would like to marry, even if one would have me!"

Jeremiah shook his head, his face troubled. He pounded the nails into the step, then stopped and looked up at her earnestly. "It isn't right, Leah. It is admirable that you raise your siblings, but what about your own life? There's only one person whose opinion really matters. If He wants you to be a wife, then He will provide a way, He will provide for your siblings, and it won't matter one whit if the banker's wife doesn't approve. You shouldn't let your life be dictated by others' opinions, only God's. You are a beautiful, young woman. Any man should feel the luckiest in all of California to have you for his wife."

One word completely overshadowed the rest of his encouragement, and it would be a while before Leah could even recall the rest of his speech.

Leah must have heard wrong. Did he say she was… "Beautiful?"

Jeremiah looked slightly uncomfortable, and… was that a blush? Looking down at the step, he tested it with the toe of his shoe.

"Yes, beautiful, and loving, and generous, and godly, and…" he swallowed with difficulty, then raised his eyes to meet hers, tentatively, like a little boy nervously asking for a forbidden piece of candy. "Beautiful."

He paused, letting the full weight of the word fall.

Then he blinked. "And, no. I haven't been in the West long enough to think all women, being so few and far between, are beautiful."

Jeremiah broke eye contact and tapped the step a few more times with the hammer. "Now it's your turn. What do you need to talk to me about?"

Leah breathed. On the one hand, she was grateful for the change of subject. She had no idea how to react to his attention. It was inconceivable that a gentleman, let alone a minister would find her attractive and admirable. On the other hand, she didn't know if she could collect her scattered thoughts to speak coherently. Or even if she wanted to.

She should just tell him and get it over with. She should inform him of what she overheard, and let him make the judgment on whether the congregation's actions were objectionable.

Then an awful thought struck her. Jeremiah thought she was an admirable woman, even though she'd done little to earn his high opinion. But there was no way for her to tell him about the mail order bride, without revealing how she got the information.

She'd overheard. She hadn't been told or included in the meeting. She had snuck around the back of the church and deliberately listened when she wasn't supposed to. Was eavesdropping a sin? If Jeremiah knew what she'd done, would he think less of her?

With a pit in her stomach, she remembered what Jeremiah had said earlier about how it would be wrong if she spread secrets and gossip about her observations. But telling him what the congregation was planning wouldn't be doing that, or would it?

Lord, what should I do?

She watched Jeremiah test the step again, making sure it was secure.

He was a good man who wanted to help. She wouldn't feel right about not telling him, even if it made her look bad.

Leah cleared her throat. "I went to clean the church last night, after the children were in bed. I saw—"

"Leah, why didn't you tell me the preacher came to call!" a big voice boomed.

Leah's father sauntered out of the house, marched up to Jeremiah, and stuck out his hand.

Jeremiah shook his hand, and Leah admired him even more. With only a small, telltale twitch in his cheek, the pastor successfully ignored the nauseating smell of alcohol and the fact that Henry Barton was clad only in his long underwear.

"I wouldn't expect a preacher to come calling this early in the day," he said good-naturedly. "He may find his parishioners indisposed."

"I apologize, Mr. Barton," Jeremiah said easily. "I was just helping your daughter with young Curtis, who came home sick from school. I must be going now for another appointment, but perhaps we could arrange another time for you and me to have a proper visit."

Henry squinted his eyes in the bright sun. "Well, I'll have to get back to you on that, Reverend. My schedule is mighty busy these days."

Jeremiah nodded. "I understand."

"Pa, maybe you should go inside," Leah suggested, feeling humiliation flood over her in wave after wave. If the bright red underwear weren't embarrassing enough, he also wore boots and a dilapidated bowler hat. His eyes were overly bright and his scraggly whiskers needed a shave months ago.

"Nonsense, child!" He rasped, moving to perch on the step Jeremiah had just repaired. He stood with his hands on his hips in all his underwear glory, looking out at the trees, basking in the warmth of the sunshine. "A beautiful day like today is meant to be enjoyed outside!"

"I must be going, Miss Barton," Jeremiah said. He bent to pick something and then stood back up, handing Leah a delicate blue wildflower that had been hiding beside the step. "Thank you for the meal. I won't forget that you owe me a conversation."

Leah took the flower and managed a soft smile.

Jeremiah turned and walked to the road, passing Johnny's project on the way. "You're working mighty hard, Johnny," Leah heard him say.

Johnny looked up, his smile bright. "It's a trap for a deer," he said excitedly. "Leah won't let me use Pa's gun. But I think I can catch one this way."

Jeremiah turned around to wave to Hazel and took a step.

But instead of meeting the ground, his foot kept going.

Leah watched in horror as he toppled through the leaves into a large hole they'd been disguising.

Leah ran, praying Jeremiah was okay, while Johnny hopped up and down excitedly. "It works! It works!"

Reaching the edge of the hole, Leah peered down to see the reverend flat on his back in a pit of black ooze. His feet were completely buried and his face, his suit, and even his hair were almost unrecognizable. Looking up with a sheepish grin, he announced, "Looks like I found the manure!"

Chapter 5

"Shhh!" Leah whispered fiercely.

This was such a bad idea. She knew it. She'd known it the instant it popped into her head. And yet here she was.

Hiding in the loft of the livery.

Waiting to eavesdrop on a church member meeting.

With three children in tow.

Footsteps sounded from below. Leah made Curtis and Johnny sit down in the hay, handing them each a stick. With her pantomimed gestures, they figured out she expected them to whittle and stay quiet. By her stern looks, she also hoped they understood the serious consequences if they did not keep silent.

For Hazel, she took out the girl's collection of stick dolls, thankful that she kept them in her bag. Hazel began to play, and Leah carefully sat down on the hay beside her, trying not to make any noise that would alert those below to their presence.

"Are you sure the preacher won't come by?" someone whispered worriedly.

"No, he's over working on the church," another voice reported. "I saw him swingin' his hammer right before I came in here. We should be safe."

Leah hadn't seen much of Jeremiah Moore the past month for that very reason. He had taken a lot of church repairs upon himself, wanting to complete the projects before winter. Other than a nod at church or a few long looks exchanged in the mercantile while he was conversing with someone else, she hadn't encountered him at all.

"Is everyone here?" another voice asked.

"I don't know. I think this is good enough. I don't have all evening."

And with that last line, Leah recognized Mrs. Beagle's voice.

"How many have had the opportunity to read all of the letters? We've been trying to pass them around, but there are quite a few."

Leah was sure that was Mr. Tuft speaking. She wished she could actually see the group gathered below, but she didn't think there was a way to get a better angle. She was fortunate to have made it in time for the meeting at all. Leah had seen Mrs. Beagle receive letters at the mercantile for the past few weeks, but didn't know when the congregation was planning to meet again. Less than an hour ago, she'd been in the mercantile with the three children, delivering eggs, when she'd seen Frankie Smithers conversing with Mr. Tuft. Frankie was not the subtle sort, and from his repeated furtive glances around the store, it certainly looked like he was hiding something. He was also not the quiet sort. While Leah pretended interest in some thread, she clearly overheard Frankie tell Mr. Tuft that he thought he'd gotten word to everybody to meet at the livery at 4:00.

Glancing at the clock, Leah realized that was less than fifteen minutes away! Having nowhere to take the children and no time to develop a plan, Leah dragged them with her to the livery. She needed to know what the congregation was planning. She had spent the last month berating herself over not telling Jeremiah, and she hadn't had another chance. Her only hope was that if she was able to get more information, she would know what to do. Maybe the congregation wouldn't find a bride at all, in which case it would be pointless to tell Jeremiah.

So she had pushed the children up the ladder to the loft, and then hiked up her skirts and climbed up after them. She didn't know if it was right or not, but it was too late to change her mind. For better or worse, she was eavesdropping on a church society meeting again, and as much as she would like to actually spy on them, for now she would have to be content with just hearing the voices.

"The choice is clear." Mrs. Beagle's voice was slightly bored and irritated. "Let's take a vote and be done. If I send a telegram right away, we should have her here within a month, maybe as soon as two weeks. There's no sense wasting time. Wouldn't you agree, Mr. Beagle?"

"Now, Winifred, that isn't right," Mr. Tuft objected. "Not everyone has read the letters yet to be able to give an opinion."

Mrs. Beagle sniffed. "Well, I'm sure those who *can* read, would agree with my assessment. We could read them aloud for everyone, but the end result would be the same. Mr. Beagle has read the letters and firmly agrees. Like I said, there is one clear candidate."

"If you would have turned the letters over as you received them, this wouldn't be an issue." Mr. Tuft's voice was tight. "Instead, you kept them to yourself until yesterday. That didn't give us enough time to be ready for this meeting."

"I put the only one that mattered on top. Do you wish me to read that one to everyone?" Mrs. Beagle asked sweetly. "Then we can get on with the vote."

"Which one are you talkin' 'bout, Mrs. Beagle?" Frankie's voice chimed in. "When I read the letters, I saw a couple that seemed like nice young ladies."

"I'm referring to Begonia Hardesty, of course. She answered the advertisement in the newspaper back East."

"Ain't she the one from that fancy girls' school?" Frankie asked doubtfully.

"Yes, she is," Mrs. Beagle confidently replied. "She is a lady of class and quality. She attended a ladies' finishing school and was provided a thorough education in womanly arts. She is the perfect candidate to be our pastor's wife."

At Mrs. Beagle's description, Leah felt indignation, along with a strange streak of jealousy. She really didn't think that Jeremiah would want a high society wife, but maybe that's what gentlemen liked. What Leah would give to be a real lady!

"She'd fit in here like a fishing pole in the desert!" Frankie objected. "I liked the one in San Francisco. She seemed a nice, sensible sort, used to hard work. And I could go down to fetch her and be back in a few days."

"Miss Cox?" Mrs. Beagle sputtered. "Why she's nothing but a farm girl! I'm sure she's adequate, but not when you have a bride of the quality of Begonia Hardesty."

Hearing a rustling sound, Leah looked over to see her brothers tagging each other back and forth.

She snapped her fingers, trying to get their attention.

Stop it! She mouthed.

Having tired of their whittling, they were now seeking other ways to entertain themselves. Leah hoped the meeting would hurry up. She didn't know how much longer she could keep the boys quiet.

"Frankie has a point, Winifred." Mr. Tuft said. "This isn't New York. Miss Hardesty's fancy skills would likely be wasted around here."

Mr. Tuft's comment was met with several grunts of agreement. "Don't want no prissy flower who can't get her hands dirty," another voice said.

"That Miss Cox seems like she could put in a hard day's work," Frankie said, his tone one of admiration. "And didn't she say somethin' about bein' a preacher's daughter?"

That strange surge of jealousy shot through Leah again. Miss Cox did sound like a good woman, one the reverend might appreciate. Leah was a hard worker too, but she certainly didn't have the admirable pedigree of either Miss Hardesty or Miss Cox.

Mrs. Beagle snorted. "She'll be a minister's wife. A hard day's work won't be necessary. We need a lady—a woman who can help our town grow in prestige and estimation."

"Nonsense! We need a hard-working woman who knows how to help care for a household and a frontier community. Miss Hardesty likely wouldn't survive a winter in the Sierras. But Miss Cox could chop wood and build a fire herself."

Feeling a tug on her sleeve, Leah looked down to see Hazel looking up at her, her features scrunched and miserable.

"Leah," Hazel whispered. "I need to go!"

By the look on her face, Leah knew exactly what the four-year-old was referring to. Hazel needed an outhouse. And she needed it now.

But the argument down below wasn't showing any signs of wrapping up.

"It is my money," Mrs. Beagle said firmly. "I refuse to allow it to be spent on a less-than-worthy wife."

Frankie shot right back, "You don't need to spend a penny of your precious money if we get Miss Cox from San Francisco!"

There were exactly two seconds of taut silence before Mrs. Beagle spoke, her tone allowing no further argument. "The decision has been made. And Mr. Beagle agrees. I am the head of this society, I will make the call. I will telegram Miss Hardesty first thing tomorrow."

But Frankie would have none of it. "You don't run this town, or this church, Mrs. Beagle. And I don't think the good reverend would 'preciate you ordering him some fancy bride the rest of the church doesn't want, just so you can have company at tea time!"

Leah took Hazel's hand and moved quietly to the ladder. Johnny and Curtis, really bored now, followed behind. Unfortunately, Leah didn't think there was any way to get down from the loft without being seen.

"Can you wait just a few minutes?" she whispered to her sister.

The little girl adamantly shook her blonde head. "I gotta go now!"

Maybe everyone would be so engrossed in the argument they wouldn't notice. The big hay stack sat right beside the ladder. If they could just get down the ladder without attracting attention, they could hide behind the haystack and then bolt for the door directly across.

"Frankie Smithers, you would do well to remember who it is who pays your salary! Mr. Beagle, didn't you say just the other day that there was another gentleman who was interested in employment?"

"Winifred, wait." Mr. Tuft's calming voice entered the conversation, immediately diffusing some of the tension. "Let's not say anything we will regret. And making threats doesn't do us any good. Winifred, you agreed that we would all have a part in this, not just you. How about we vote. I know not everyone has read the letters, but you've heard the discussion. Mrs. Beagle believes Miss Begonia Hardesty of New York is the best candidate. Frankie Smithers believes Miss Amy Cox, a farm girl most recently in San Francisco, is the one we need as our pastor's wife. If we could get a show of hands…"

Leah put her foot on the top rung of the ladder.

There were murmurs and grunts of approval.

"Who wants to vote for Miss Hardesty?"

Silence

"And Miss Cox?"

More silence.

"That certainly looks like an even split."

"So what do we do now?" Frankie asked.

Feeling a sharp jab in the back, Leah turned to see her brothers continuing their game of tag. Though they were silent, they were covering more distance. Curtis reached out and tapped Johnny on the arm. Johnny reached out to return the tap, but Curtis danced away from his outstretched fingers.

"I'm the one who started this society and funded the advertisements, my vote should be worth more," Mrs. Beagle asserted. "And since Mr. Beagle is the unofficial mayor of Secret, since he's the banker and owns the most land, his vote should be worth more too. And fortunately, both Mr. Beagle and I agree on a candidate!"

"That ain't right!" Frankie protested.

"Boys!" Leah hissed, trying to get her brothers' attention.

Leah heard the sound of a throat delicately clearing and for an instant, she worried her admonition had been heard.

But then a soft voice spoke, "Since we are a church society. And we are talking about the reverend's wife, shouldn't we pray about it? I'm not quite sure why there is a big rush. Maybe we should take some time and ask the good Lord which lady He would have us send for?"

Leah was sure that was Mrs. Tuft's voice of reason and really wanted to applaud for the soft-spoken woman.

"That seems like a good bit of wisdom right there." Frankie said. "We don't have to decide for sure today."

"Why don't we all take some time to pray and meet back here at the beginning of next month?" Mr.

Tuft instructed. "That will give everyone a chance to go over the letters and seek the Lord's will in this."

Hazel pulled on her sleeve again, and Leah looked down to see the girl dancing uncomfortably.

She desperately wanted to get Hazel down the ladder, but with the turn of the conversation, she knew they would be seen for sure.

"I'm pretty sure the Lord gave us intelligence enough to be able to use common sense," Mrs. Beagle sniffed. "A woman like Begonia Hardesty won't wait around forever. If we don't snatch her up for Secret, someone else will!"

Leah heard more rustling and looked back to see Johnny and Curtis at it again. Johnny reached for Curtis, who danced away, almost bumping into Leah and Hazel.

"If that happens, then we will for sure know she wasn't for us," Mr. Tuft said wisely. "If she is still around when and if the committee decides she's our gal, then we can take that to mean the good Lord saved her for us."

Sidestepping another swipe, Curtis stepped back. But he was at the edge of the loft. His heel went back and his weight went with it. Teetering on the rim, Leah lunged forward, trying to grab him. But she missed. Her hand caught air and with the sudden momentum, her own foot slipped on the hay.

"I tell you, I won't stand for it! I'm not about to let a bunch of ignorant—"

Feeling herself falling, Leah shrieked. Her legs went over her head in a somersault.

Umph!

Landing in the big pile of hay, her breath knocked out in a rush, the only painful part being Curtis's foot in her ribs.

Not taking time to even catch her breath, she scrambled down from the haystack and ran to the ladder. After helping Hazel down, she turned to her audience. "I apologize for the interruption," she said with as much grace as one can muster when covered in hay. "If you will excuse me, we have an emergency of sorts."

With no further explanation, Leah picked Hazel up and hurried her outside to the outhouse. Trying desperately not to think of what had just happened, she plopped Hazel on the hole, shut the door to the outhouse, and waited.

Despite her efforts, the image of all of the church members staring at her with shocked expressions and open mouths wouldn't leave her mind. She was so humiliated!

After approximately two seconds, Hazel hopped off the bench and screeched open the door to the outhouse.

"All done!" she announced.

"That was it?" Leah asked. "I thought you had to go really bad."

"I did!" Hazel replied, seeming offended.

Leah shut her eyes, took a deep breath, and counted to three.

How she wished she didn't have to go back inside the livery. She really wanted to run away and hide until everyone forgot that she'd just interrupted a church society meeting by tumbling out of the livery loft while eavesdropping. But she had to go back inside to claim Johnny and Curtis, so escape was not really an option.

With a prayer for strength, she marched back inside with Hazel in tow. On the tip of her tongue was another heartfelt apology, but Frankie spoke as soon as she came through the door.

"Miss Leah, I was just telling everyone how I let Johnny and Curtis here play in the loft. They sure like jumpin' off into that pile of hay, and I ain't never seen no harm in it."

Bless him! Frankie was trying to help.

"Well, I own this livery, and I do see the harm in it!" Mrs. Beagle spat. "I don't suppose they care one whit about breaking a limb, but I'm more concerned about the huge mess it makes, spreading hay over everything."

"Nah, those boys play, but I put them to work. They clean far more than they mess up. That Curtis is great with a broom, and Johnny is as good as a man with a shovel."

Mrs. Beagle huffed, "Well, even if I liked that excuse, which I don't, that explains the children. But Miss Barton, exactly how old are you? I'm fairly certain you left childhood behind a while ago. I never knew a woman of your age who practiced jumping into haystacks."

Leah's throat was tight, and there was no way to describe her complete embarrassment. She kept her eyes downcast, afraid that the sobs would escape if she saw everyone looking at her with curiosity and accusation. Frankie had tried to help, but there was no one here who believed she was up there in the loft by accident.

Her mind flitted through possible responses to Mrs. Beagle. She didn't want to lie, but she also didn't feel the need to make a full confession. All of them were sneaking around behind the pastor's back, supposedly doing it for his own good. She was sneaking behind their backs for the exact same reason. She hadn't hurt anyone or done anything illegal, so she really didn't need to explain or justify herself, especially to the woman who seemed to take delight in insulting others.

Adopting her sweetest, most innocent expression, Leah answered softly, "How would one improve if she didn't practice, Mrs. Beagle? If you are interested, I'm sure Mr. Smithers wouldn't mind me giving you some lessons."

Frankie coughed, thinly disguising an outright guffaw of laughter. Giggles, grunts, and plain laughter spread through the rest of the group.

Mrs. Beagle's mouth opened and closed like a fish.

Mr. Tuft, unabashedly grinning, raised his voice to the group. "I think we're done for the night, folks. Frankie and I will make sure all the letters make the rounds to be read. We all need to say our prayers about which bride to choose. We will meet back here in three or four weeks to vote. I'll let you know the exact time and date. Shall we close in prayer?"

Though she really wanted to watch the others, Leah resisted the temptation and closed her eyes. She appreciated them praying. So far, it was the only thing about this whole situation that made her think things might actually turn out right. If they were seeking God's will, then maybe Jeremiah Moore really would end up with the right bride.

With head bowed, Mr. Tuft prayed a short and simple prayer. "Heavenly Father, we ask that you help Reverend Moore get the right wife. Give us patience with each other, and help us to know which woman You want us to choose for Secret. Amen."

After the echoes of "Amen," everyone began filing out of the livery.

Strangely, none of the looks shot her direction were accusatory. Everyone seemed not to have noticed that she never answered the question as to why she'd been in the loft. Instead, she was given nods and smiles of appreciation.

"Miss Barton, may I have a word with you?" Mrs. Beagle was at her elbow, sending her a clear look that said, though she had phrased her statement as a question, she really wasn't giving Leah an option to refuse.

"Of course," Leah said, though she desperately looked around for any excuse or help. But Frankie was talking with Mr. Tuft, and neither realized she'd been ambushed by Mrs. Beagle.

Looking at the children, she saw a smiling Mr. Beagle talking to them. Much to their delight, he pulled out peppermint sticks and presented one to each of them. Though completely domineered by his wife, Mr. Beagle was a very kind man when left to his own devices. But his kindness to her siblings had just eliminated Leah's last chance of an excuse.

"Miss Barton, let me warn you not to discuss what you overheard with Reverend Moore." Coming directly to the point, Mrs. Beagle's words were bitten out from tense lips.

Leah supposed she could pretend that she didn't understand what the woman was talking about, but she knew she wouldn't be believed for an instant.

"Reverend Moore deserves to be told if you are sending for him a bride," Leah said firmly, deciding to match Mrs. Beagle's direct attitude with her own. "In fact, he deserves to be allowed to choose a bride for himself."

"Nonsense! We know what kind of preacher's wife we need in this community. We are doing this for his benefit. If we consulted him, he would consider it a matter of pride and not allow us to handle the costs. This is our gift to him. As a church congregation, we've agreed. And since you are not a member, I ask, no I demand, that you stay out of it!"

"You demand?"

"Yes! I am not ignorant enough to think that you were up there in the loft by accident or because you were playing. You were snooping. And no one likes a snoop. If you find it your duty to tell Reverend Moore of his gift, then I may find it my duty to let certain other people in our community know of your affinity for snooping."

"Is that a threat, Mrs. Beagle?" Leah asked, completely shocked.

"Of course not, Miss Barton," she said, her nose scrunching up as if even the thought was offensive. "If I was going to threaten, I'd remind you that your home is rented space on my property. I would hate to have something happen that would endanger your home. With your siblings to care for, you wouldn't want them out in the cold with nowhere to go, especially with autumn upon us. It might be especially difficult if your employment were to suffer as well. Of course, I would do everything I could, since I'm on the church board, to treat your employment justly. And though I know others in town don't care for employees who snoop, I would want to do what was fair by you, even though word travels very fast in Secret. I imagine a reputation of being a snoop would be difficult to overcome, especially with someone of your particular background."

Leah swallowed with difficulty. Mrs. Beagle's message couldn't be more clear. "I understand. Reverend Moore won't hear about his bride from me."

Working to choke back tears, Leah took the hands of Hazel and Curtis and walked out of the livery with Johnny trailing along behind. She tried to hold her head up high, but couldn't quite manage it. Any hope she'd harbored to be someone more, to do something important, to do the right thing, had just been snuffed out and replaced with humiliation.

With her eyes to the hay-strewn floor, she left without making eye contact with anyone.

The cold air hit her hot cheeks in a rush, but she ignored the sting and hurried the children along to the two-room shack waiting silent and cold on property that didn't belong to them.

She would never be allowed to be anything more that Leah Barton, destitute daughter of the Secret town drunk.

And what made that hurt even worse was knowing that Reverend Moore, a good man she couldn't help but admire, was soon to be the recipient of a bride of the congregation's choice.

And, since she was just Leah Barton, there was absolutely nothing she could do about it.

Chapter 6

"Miss Barton!"

Leah clearly heard the call. And she recognized the voice.

But she ignored it. She kept her eyes straight ahead, pretending, as she had for the past month, that she didn't even know a man named Jeremiah Moore.

She hurried down the street, hoping to duck out of sight before the reverend caught up to her. She had successfully avoided him this long, hopefully she could do it again.

The only problem was that this was the first time he had deliberately sought her out. So far, avoidance had involved cleaning the church at hours when she knew he wouldn't be there, hiding on the other side of the mercantile when he visited, and leaving immediately following Sunday service. Other than a few curious gazes sent her direction, from which she had quickly averted her eyes, she'd managed no contact at all.

Though she really did long for the company of someone who didn't judge her based on her father's actions, she told herself things were better this way. She didn't trust herself not to say anything to Reverend Moore about the congregation's covert plans. On the one hand, she couldn't handle the guilt if her family was left homeless because she had informed on Mrs. Beagle's secret. On the other hand, the sheer guilt of not telling Reverend Moore made her not trust herself. He deserved to know, but because of what was at stake, her fear was too great to overcome.

She had made herself ill with worry, trying to find a solution that would keep her family safe and do what was right by Reverend Moore, but she hadn't found one. Instead, all she could do was avert her eyes whenever he looked her way, and as the situation warranted now, run down the street in the opposite direction.

Recent rain had made one side of the street extra muddy. Not wanting to be slowed down by picking her way through, Leah tightly clutched her delivery of eggs and swerved suddenly to cross the street. A wagon turned a corner at the same time, but the driver was looking back toward the train tracks, and didn't see Leah. With a strangled cry, Leah dove for the side of the road, landing in a puddle. The mixture of mud, manure, and water instantly soaked through her cloak and dress. Leah rolled off her front and pushed herself into a sitting position. Her breath caught in a sob at the sight of yellow streams of egg swirling through the brown concoction like eggs freshly cracked into chocolate cake batter.

"Miss Barton!"

Leah didn't check to see how close Jeremiah was. She already knew he would be rushing to her rescue. Not even thinking through how it would look, she dragged herself to her feet and dashed around the corner of the nearest building.

Leah sniffled and held her breath, trying to control the sobs. She knew she was not acting reasonably. Jeremiah had seen her. And he had seen her dive into the puddle. She was only making things worse by running away. But she couldn't help it. He was the last person in Secret who seemed to hold a good opinion of her, especially after her last escapade with the haystack in the livery. She couldn't handle the thought of losing that good opinion. No matter how nice and godly Jeremiah was, no one could carry a favorable opinion of a woman covered in yuck who also happened to be harboring a secret that could ruin your life.

Unfortunately, Leah couldn't run very far. Her dress was heavy with water, and her shoes were so soaked and caked with mud that her escape soon left her panting for breath. She rounded a corner to the back of the building and pressed herself against the rough logs at her back. She waited, breathing heavily and praying that Jeremiah wouldn't follow. Maybe he hadn't seen exactly where she'd gone.

Then she looked down at the ground and groaned. Even if, by some miracle he hadn't seen her, all he had to do was follow the muddy egg-water trail she had dripped behind her.

Footsteps hurried along the side of the building. Leah fought against the shivers coursing through her body. Every day the temperature was colder than the last. Soon the rain would be snow and the puddles would be sheets of ice.

Unable to still the shaking, she held her breath, listening to the steps coming closer. He would round the corner any second.

"Reverend Moore!" a new voice called.

The footsteps stopped.

"Could I borrow you for a moment? My Bessie isn't feeling so well, and I would sure 'preciate a prayer."

Leah felt Jeremiah hesitate. She imagined him looking around for her, his eyes sweeping the space between this building and the next. She held perfectly still, not even allowing breath to raise her chest.

"Certainly," Reverend Moore finally replied. "I'm sure I can spare a few moments to pray for someone in need."

Footsteps sounded back down the other way, growing fainter by the second. Leah's breath came out in a rush. Cautiously, she picked her way around the back of the next building. Seeing the way clear, she dashed to the next one as well. As quickly as she could, she made her way home, making her own route by way of the back of the buildings. She hoped she could make it safely into their house without being seen and before Jeremiah figured out that the poor, sick Bessie needing prayer was Milo Pope's mean, old mule.

Ten minutes later, a wet and thoroughly chilled Leah opened the door of her empty house, thankful that Mrs. Pope had consented to watch Hazel while she delivered the eggs. Since she didn't have a large wardrobe, Leah made quick work of changing out of her filthy work dress and putting on the only other dress she owned, her Sunday best. If she worked quickly, she might be able to get her work dress clean and let it dry overnight in front of the fire to have it dry for tomorrow. She really didn't want to wear her Sunday best to work in. Besides being a shade of green that flattered her eyes and the subtle auburn tints in her hair, it was special. It had been her mother's dress. With barely enough money to pay for rent and food, Leah had to be content with two dresses. And that was usually fine, but not when one encountered a puddle of the magnitude Leah had.

Leah mentally calculated how long it would take to wash her dress, and debated whether she should do it before or after she picked up Hazel from Mrs. Pope's house.

A knock sounded on the door.

Still clutching the soiled dress in her hands, she hesitantly opened the door.

Jeremiah stood there, his brow furrowed in concern.

"Are you all right?" he asked immediately. "I saw you fall. I tried to hurry to your aid, but you must not have heard me. Then I was delayed by a... prayer request. Were you injured?"

"No, I am fine," Leah quickly assured. "I had to choose an encounter with a puddle or a wagon, and I chose the puddle."

"Good choice," he replied. But instead of asking or saying something else, he just looked at her. His silent study made her nervous. He was so intent, and yet Leah felt so awkward, she didn't know where to look. Why was he looking at her that way? Did he know she was keeping a secret? Should she say something? What did he want anyway?

"Was there something else that I could help you with?" Leah finally asked, unable to take his silent study any longer.

Jeremiah blinked and looked away, his trance broken. "Oh, yes. I apologize. I should have mentioned it sooner. I was just distracted with concern after witnessing your fall."

His gaze returned again to hers, and she could now read sadness. Her heart leapt. Something was wrong.

"Jolly is asking for you," he said quietly.

Leah's breath caught. "Is she...?"

Jeremiah nodded. "I don't think it will be long now. Doc thinks sometime in the next two days she'll see the gates of heaven."

Leah nodded. "I'll go right away. Let me just..." She turned around, not even sure what she needed to do first. The news of her dear friend threw her off so much that her mind was running in circles. Jolly was the only person in Secret who loved her. She'd always treated her well, not caring about her father's reputation, and had become almost a grandmother to her younger siblings.

"Let's see, the boys are at school, but I need to go pick up Hazel from Mrs. Pope's house."

Jeremiah nodded. "I hope you don't mind, but I already took care of that. Mr. Pope was the one who'd requested prayer, so I was already at their house and saw Hazel. I asked if Mrs. Pope would mind watching her a little longer so you could go make your goodbyes with Jolly. She very kindly agreed."

"Oh, thank you for taking care of that," Leah said, relieved. "Hazel loves Jolly, but I think it would be very upsetting to see her so very ill and have to say goodbye."

"Jolly asked that you come alone," Jeremiah confirmed. "She doesn't want the children to be upset."

Leah felt tears prick her eyes. That was so very like the kind woman. Here she was dying and still thinking about others!

Leah grabbed her coat and followed Jeremiah out the door. Her father was likely still asleep in the bedroom, but there was no reason to disturb him.

She would be back before he woke up and Johnny and Curtis returned from school.

"Let me put the chickens back in their coop before I go," she said, immediately shooing the birds that direction. She had let them out this morning, but didn't feel comfortable leaving them for longer than the hour it usually took to deliver her eggs and accomplish her town errands. There were too many predators in the mountains, and with the eggs breaking this morning, she couldn't afford to lose a single hen. In order for the children to have eggs for breakfast in the morning and also have enough for her orders, she would need all the hens to lay."

The good reverend helped chase a few wayward chickens back into the coop, and Leah was soon setting the latch.

"I wondered how you managed to keep chickens with the wild animals and cold mountain weather. It looks like you have quite the system, though."

"Well, it isn't fancy, but it works," Leah smiled with a trace of pride. "See how the coop is pushed right next to the house? There is a hole that connects the two with a screen in between. That way the chickens can't get into the house, but the heat can warm the coop in the winter."

"That's smart. No wonder your eggs are in demand."

Leah nodded, pleased that he'd noticed. "Many people didn't think I'd be able to keep the chickens alive in the winter. But I do. Their laying slows down considerably, but then they pick back up in the spring." Those chickens helped put food on their table in more than one way and she was proud to have a successful business, no matter how small it was. It had been her idea to keep chickens to earn money after their mother passed away. When others expressed serious doubts about keeping them alive in such a harsh place as the Sierra Mountains, Leah had cut a hole in the side of their house herself and fitted it with a screen.

She only wished they would continue laying through the winter. She was hiding every penny she earned, hoping it would be enough to make it through the lean winter months ahead. Others in the congregation may have felt the amount of prayer Leah devoted to those chickens to be sacrilegious. But, even as she followed Jeremiah away from the house, she silently prayed that God would allow Genesis, Proverbs, and Habakkuk to all lay eggs tomorrow.

Leah's thoughts soon drifted to Jolly, and her prayers shifted as well. She was so deep in thought and prayer that she didn't really notice the silence as she walked with Jeremiah down the worn trail.

While the Barton's house was closer to town, Jolly's place sat on the claim she and her husband had worked before his death. The claim was about a ten minute walk the opposite direction from town, down a trail that tunneled through a forest of trees.

Their footfalls on the path were muted by a blanket of leaves and pine needles as they walked side by side. With the diffused light of autumn filtering through the canopy overhead, the trail was bathed in a soft, golden glow in what should have been a breathtaking setting.

However, the beauty was largely lost on Leah, and had she not been so engrossed in her own thoughts and prayers, she might have noticed the tension threading the silence. And maybe she wouldn't have been so startled when Jeremiah suddenly stopped and turned a slightly accusatory gaze on her.

"Leah, have I done something to offend you?"

Shock sizzled through her body. "N-No!" Leah stammered. "Of course not!"

"Then why have you been avoiding me for the last month?"

Chapter 7

Leah gagged, her throat suddenly too dry to get any air through. "Reverend Moore," she rasped breathlessly. "I'm not..." But she couldn't lie to him. Besides being wrong, it had to be extra wrong to lie to a minister.

"It's Jeremiah," he said with a frown. "Remember?"

Leah nodded, but shut her eyes, trying to focus on a way to explain. "Jeremiah, I can't..."

"Leah, is this about your father?"

Leah's eyes flew open. "My father?"

"I may have only come to Secret recently, but I know more than you think I do. I know that your family came to Secret for the same reason as everyone else—mining. Your pa had a claim that he worked, and then, two years ago, your mother passed away. Since then, your father has spent nearly every night at the saloon, while the responsibility for providing for your family and caring for your siblings fell to you. Your father lost his claim, the rumor is that he gambled it away. Now you live on land owned by the Beagles." There was no judgment in his voice, just facts.

"That is all true," Leah said, bravely meeting his eyes. But the compassion she saw was nearly her undoing, and she looked away. She didn't know which was worse, derision or pity, but she wanted neither from Jeremiah.

"Leah, I know that not everyone in Secret is respectful or kind to you, but that isn't right. You should not be punished for your father's sins. From what I've seen, you are an admirable woman who should hold her head high."

"Thank you for saying so, Jeremiah, but as you said, not everyone feels the way you do. Most people seem to also view me as a child, and when combined with my father's actions, that makes me unfit to be in the respectable category."

"So is that why you've been avoiding me? Because you're afraid what people will say if they saw me keeping company with you?"

That was not the reason. But he did make a very valid point. If Reverend Moore was to show her attention of more than just a passing nature, then that could be problematic for both of them. Should she bother disagreeing, or just go along with his reasoning on the subject?

Leah replied hesitantly, "I do not reflect well on you, and I don't want to get you in trouble, especially with the Beagles working to bring more refinement to Secret. I don't expect you to give my family or me any attention other than a nod our direction on Sundays. I understand the predicament, and I'm fine with it."

"But I'm not!" Jeremiah said adamantly. Eyes flashing, Jeremiah strode back and forth in front of her. With his exaggerated hand motions and impassioned voice, he looked as if he could be delivering a most fiery sermon. "Leah, the only person's opinion that matters is God's. If I let other people's hypocritical opinions dictate my actions, then I would be wrong. I will not simply nod at any person in need, and I will not live my life in fear of what others may think, or say, or do. In the end, I answer to God and Him only. I will seek to follow God's Word and act accordingly."

"I appreciate that… "

"But?"

"Maybe it's pride…" Leah bit her lip, not sure if she should even say it. But then the words came out as if of their own volition. "I don't want to be your charity case!"

Jeremiah smiled and stepped toward her. Gently, he took one of her cold hands in his. "I am a minister, but I am still a man. The Bible speaks of friends and enjoying life. I think I'm still entitled to do some of that—to have a life, enjoy it, and give God the glory for every blessing He sends my way. I was never speaking of you in terms of a charity case. Yes, I want to help you however I can, but I do believe my interest extends further than pure philanthropy or religious duty."

Leah swallowed, her heart beating wildly. She was reading too much into Jeremiah's words. He'd mentioned friends. That had to be it. He admired her. Wanted her as a friend. He was not interested in more than friendship. He couldn't be.

There was no way he was attracted to her.

The way she was to him.

He couldn't feel the same sparks at the touch of their clasped hands. His breathing didn't catch at the sensation of his warm breath brushing her face. He didn't wonder what it would feel like if his lips moved down just a little more to meet hers...

Leah stepped back. As if coming up for air after swimming in a lake, she struggled to get her bearings.

"Jolly must be waiting. I feel bad. I don't want to keep her waiting. How long did the doctor think she has? Maybe she's been waiting too long." Leah knew she was babbling. She'd said "waiting" three times already, and her mind was already thinking up a few more to add to the count.

With an amused grin, Jeremiah held up his hand to stop her words. "Jolly isn't waiting. I should have told you sooner. She was sleeping when I left. She told me to come back at 2:00 with you." He took out his pocket watch. "It looks like we're right on schedule."

They walked the rest of the way in silence. Leah's hand swung at her side and felt strangely bereft without the warmth of Jeremiah's. She sidled a few glances his direction, and to her embarrassment, he caught her every time with his own amused gaze. She quickly looked away, but felt warmth moving up her face and increasing in hue with every attempt.

She shouldn't be feeling this way. She was on her way to say goodbye to her dying friend, the woman who'd been the closest thing Leah had to a mother since her own had passed away. And yet here she was, feeling things she should definitely not be feeling. And for a pastor!

The trees parted to reveal a small house nestled on Jolly's claim. Though it wasn't bigger than Leah's house, it was considerably better constructed. While Jolly's husband hadn't struck it rich, as he had hoped, he had succeeded enough to build their little house. Though Jolly didn't have much, Leah suspected that she had squirreled enough away to help provide for basic necessities after he had passed.

The door squeaked on its hinges as Jeremiah pulled it open to let Leah pass through.

"It's 'bout time you got here," a voice rasped.

Leah felt a return of the rosy tinge to her face, remembering why they were delayed, but she smiled. Even on her deathbed, Jolly was as spunky as ever.

"Can I get you anything, Jolly?" Leah asked, moving to sit in the rickety chair beside her bed.

"Just you, dearie," Jolly said, weakly reaching for her hand.

Leah clasped Jolly's hand in both of hers. The sight of the well-worn fingers brought tears to her eyes, and she struggled to keep them back.

Jolly's real name was Polly. But Polly Jolly, being the tongue twister that it was, shortened easily to Jolly by everyone who knew her. And her name fit. Jolly was a happy soul. She never seemed to falter, no matter what life threw her way. When her husband George came down with gold fever, they moved from back East, leaving everything and everyone, including family. She had arrived in Secret with a smile on her face and an excitement that rivaled any gold-hungry miner. She had worked beside George, mining for elusive gold, and had quickly become friends with Leah's mother, Alice. When Alice passed away, Jolly had tried to step in and help, despite her own declining health. She had taken up where Leah's mother left off, teaching Leah cooking, gardening, cleaning, sewing, and doing it all with a good attitude.

Now the hands that had done so much for her were cold, with pale, near-translucent skin stretched taut over the bones and veins.

Jolly noticed Leah's struggle. Jolly always noticed.

She let go of Leah's hand and reached up to gently touch the moisture gathering at the corner of her eye. "It's just fine to cry, dear girl. Don't hold back for me. Won't hurt my feelings none."

"I don't want you to go," Leah choked out.

"I know, dearie, but it isn't no surprise. Doc told me those lumps were serious." Jolly closed her eyes, as if resting or waiting for a wave of sickness to pass. "Don't worry 'bout me. I go to a better place. I'll see George. And I'll get to tell your mama what a fine girl she has. You're a strong one, Leah. God will get you through."

"Sometimes I think God has forgotten me," Leah confessed in a whisper. Jolly had been her only confidant for so long, that she couldn't stop the deepest parts of her soul from being laid bare in front of the loving woman. "First Mama. Now you. And pa... Jolly, I don't know how much I can take! It's been two years, and things haven't gotten better. I barely make enough money for food, and I'm not doing a good enough job taking care of the children. You say God will get me through, but how can it be when it's never-ending?"

Jolly's eyes slid shut again, and guilt washed over Leah.

"I'm sorry, Jolly. I shouldn't have said anything. I need to be taking care of you. What can I do to help?"

"You keep telling me your troubles, dear one. Just as you've always done. I don't know the answers for you, but I do know that I'll be praying for you with every last breath I have in me. And though I go, my prayers are going to stay there at God's throne, bugging him 'til he answers them. God has a plan for you, Miss Leah. Even though you can't see it yet, he is working on it more than you know."

"Thank you, Jolly," Leah whispered. "I wish I could pay you back for all the good you've done for us. Is there anything I can do for you?"

"You sent the letter, right?"

"Yes," Leah answered confidently, even though she'd already answered this same question at least fifty times in the past two months. "I addressed it to B.G. Jolly in the care of your sister, Prudence, in Pittsburg."

"You checked the post?"

"Yes, every day," Leah assured. "There is nothing."

Hating to kill the last bit of hope left in the woman, Leah offered. "Maybe we could send a telegram."

"I tried," Jolly whispered wearily. "When I wrote letters and never heard back, I sent telegram after telegram. But I still got nothin'."

"I'm so sorry, Jolly."

"There's nothing to be done for it," she sighed. Jolly's eyes slid shut wearily.

Leah studied her friend. Jolly's pale, translucent skin was framed by waves of once rich auburn hair, now dulled gray by illness. Leah knew that although Jolly was older than her mother had been, she was by no means an old woman. But her body had reached its limit early and would not have a chance to reach into old age. Her cheeks, once rosy, were now snow white. Her body, always healthy and plump, now barely raised the blankets on her bed.

"You'll need to take care of it," Jolly announced with eyes still closed.

Leah startled, but then realized that Jolly wasn't really talking to her. Her monologue had a different intended audience.

"All things work together, Lord, all things…" Jolly continued. "I guess I'm going to have to wait 'til heaven to see that with my B.G. I know it shouldn't be long now, but when I'm gone to glory, I ask You to remember my girl and that all things verse You said in Your word."

Jolly's out-loud conversations with God weren't new. She would frequently be speaking, when one suddenly realized she wasn't actually speaking to him or her; she was praying aloud what most people just prayed in their heads.

Leah waited, and eventually, Jolly turned back to her. "I shouldn't have left my B.G. Sometimes you mess up. Sometimes you choose wrong. But I sure am thankful for that 'all things verse.'"

Leah knew the story of Jolly's daughter. It was the one subject that could summon a cloud in the woman's bright eyes. When Jolly and her husband came West, they left their only daughter with Jolly's sister, just until they could get settled. Jolly's sister had married well, but had no children of her own. They thought it would be good for both

B.G. and her aunt to have the girl stay until the Jollys at least found a place to stay.

After they acquired their claim and built their little house near Secret, they sent for their daughter. But she didn't come. From what Jolly just said, Leah realized that she hadn't heard from her daughter in the entire three years since they had left. If she had been able, Leah was sure Jolly would have gone looking for her daughter. But after George died, Jolly's health had gone downhill. By the time the woman realized her daughter was lost and not going to respond, it was too late for her to travel 2,000 miles to find her.

Leah bit her lip to keep it from trembling. She wished it had turned out differently. She wanted B.G. to walk through the door to kiss her mama goodbye.

But that wasn't going to happen.

Leah reached out and trailed a gentle finger along the soft, worn cheek, as if tracing a tear that wasn't actually there. She spoke softly. "The good news is that, from what the doctor says, you can ask Him about those 'all things' fairly soon."

Jolly's mouth relaxed into a smile. "Just maybe, I'll get to know those 'all things' before you and B.G.!" Jolly laughed, but the effort brought the pain, and her laughter was quickly replaced by moans as she writhed in agony.

Jeremiah rushed forward and held her shoulders up while she drank some medicine. After a few moments, the pain subsided, and Jolly lay in a fetal position, completely exhausted.

"Go," she whispered to Leah.

"No," Leah protested. "I'll stay with you. I don't want you to be alone."

"She won't be," Jeremiah said. "Doc will return shortly with his wife, and I will stay with her as well. You have the children to care for."

Leah looked at Jolly. She couldn't seem to muster the energy to talk, but the older woman's eyes implored her to leave. Leah understood. Jolly knew Leah had watched her mother die, knew how it had affected her, and she didn't want Leah to watch her die too.

Closing her eyes, Leah prayed aloud. "Thank you for Jolly, and all she means to me, Lord. If it's Your will, I'd still like for you to heal her and let us have her a while longer. But it that isn't your plan, please ease her pain and hold her hand until you lead her to be with You. And help me. For I don't know how to manage without her."

Leah opened her eyes, now blurred from the tears streaming down her face. Sniffling down the sobs that threatened, she bent over and gently kissed Jolly's forehead.

With the words soft and barely discernable, Jolly spoke. "God blessed me with two daughters. Love... my girls."

Leah smiled through the pain of knowing this very well may be the last time she spoke with Jolly this side of heaven. "It is I who am blessed to be one of those daughters."

With one more steadying breath, she pressed on. "Goodbye, dear one," she whispered, using one of Jolly's own pet endearments. "You've had a lot of 'all things.' It's time to go enjoy all the good God has prepared for you. Thank you, Jolly. I love you."

It took all of Leah's strength to stand up tall and turn away from Jolly.

As she did so, she heard one last whisper, "Lord, take care of my Leah."

Leah hurried to the door, afraid that one last look might be her undoing.

Jeremiah followed her out. It unnerved her to know that he had heard every little personal tidbit in their conversation. But that came second to the grief that was causing her to suck in great gulps of air, trying to keep a semblance of control.

"Stay with her," Leah whispered hoarsely. "I can find my own way home."

"I will let you know…" Jeremiah said softly.

"Thank you." With an ill-concealed sob, Leah dashed for the trail and the privacy of the woods who promised not to tell when she let the grief have its way.

Leah eventually dragged herself to Mrs. Pope's house to collect Hazel. The other two boys soon arrived home as well, and Leah mechanically fixed and served a dinner of stew. After the children were in bed, Leah sat by the fire, unable to sleep. The sheer silence should have brought comfort, but instead, it left too much space for her thoughts as she relived every moment she'd experienced with Jolly.

The dancing flames eventually lulled her into a shallow sleep, but she awoke before dawn. Rising from the chair, Leah wrapped a quilt around her shoulders, and stepped outside to see a faint light above the trees in the east, breaking up the night to herald the coming dawn. She watched for a few moments, then movement caught her eye. A darker shape moved through the shadows toward the house. Simply by the movement of his lanky gait, Leah recognized Jeremiah.

He stopped right in front of her. His eyes, shrouded in the shadows of early morning, were completely unreadable.

Leah held her breath, waiting for the announcement she was sure to come.

"She's gone," Jeremiah said softly.

Leah nodded as brimming tears instantly spilled over.

Jeremiah reached for her. His strong arms came around, enfolding her with comfort and a sense of safety she had never known.

After about two seconds in Jeremiah's arms, Leah heard singing. But it wasn't the angel variety. It was quite off key, rowdy, and oh-so-familiar.

She gasped and leapt out of Jeremiah's arms, right as her father's figure sauntered into view.

Singing some raucous bar tune which was recognizable only to him, he weaved up to the door, grabbed Leah around the waist and swung her around in a circle. Then he pumped the reverend's hand vigorously before tap dancing his way into the house.

"At least he is happy when he's intoxicated," Jeremiah said with not a little humor.

"True," Leah conceded. "And some nights, that's about all I have to be thankful for."

"I can speak with him, if you'd like," Jeremiah asked kindly.

"It won't do any good," Leah said, unable to hide the sense of hopelessness in her voice.

Jeremiah nodded. "Another time then," he said formally. Then he held up a large bag Leah had not seen before. "Jolly asked me to give these to you."

Leah accepted the bag, already knowing the contents. Jolly had sent Leah her clothes. Around here, nothing went to waste, even in death.

"The funeral will be on Sunday," Jeremiah said. "People will already be gathered for the Sunday services. That will also give us a chance to prepare the grave and take care of a few legal matters. Jolly left her claim to the church."

Leah nodded, thankful she hadn't left it to Leah. The woman probably understood that it would have been a greater burden than blessing to Leah since there was no way she could work the claim herself. Hopefully the church would find a way to put it to good use.

"Thank you for coming to tell me," Leah said. "And for taking care of Jolly."

Jeremiah sighed wearily. "I have a lot to attend to. I'd best be going."

With a nod of his head, Jeremiah turned and strode away, leaving Leah feeling utterly bereft. Not only had she lost Jolly, but she also keenly felt the loss of those few seconds of comfort in Jeremiah's arms.

Long after his shadow had blended in with the dark trees, Leah stood still, watching east.

And for the first time in Leah's life, the sun came up on a world without Jolly.

Chapter 8

Something wasn't right.

The Beagles were arguing.

Leah sat in the pew behind the couple, awaiting the beginning of Sunday services. Though most of their disagreement was silent, the murderous looks of Mrs. Beagle, combined with the red hue of Mr. Beagle's flustered face, made the situation very clear.

Ever so slightly, Leah leaned forward, trying to catch just a snippet of their conversation.

"Winifred, this is not the time," Mr. Beagle was saying.

"Mr. Beagle," Mrs. Beagle hissed. "I refuse to change the plan for no reason. Reverend Moore deserves to know!"

Relief washed over Leah. Was Mrs. Beagle going to tell Jeremiah the truth about their plans for his mail order bride? It certainly sounded so!

"Excuse me," a quiet voice said.

Leah turned to look at the woman sitting beside Mrs. Beagle. Leah didn't recognize her, which wasn't overly strange. The population of Secret was always in flux, but it was more unusual to see a visitor of such fine dress. She was obviously a woman of breeding and quality, if the cut of her fashionable gown could be trusted.

Leah wondered if this was the Beagles' daughter. She knew the couple had a married daughter, but as far as Leah knew, she had never visited Secret. It seemed strange though, if this was the Beagles' daughter, she looked nothing like her parents. This woman looked much taller and more substantial than the Beagles. The Beagles were small people, and Leah always thought it fortunate that Mr. Beagle was a banker. She didn't think he could manage doing the manual labor of a farmer or miner. This woman, however, although she was beautiful, she also seemed healthy and strong. A stiff Sierra wind wouldn't likely blow her away.

Leah didn't even know for sure if this woman was with the Beagles. Sundays in Secret meant the church was packed with people sitting shoulder to shoulder in the pews. If one happened to be late, he or she might be left standing at the back for the length of the service.

While the Beagles argued, this woman was now addressing Leah, which made it seem more likely that she was not with them at all.

"Do you know where I can find George and Polly Jolly?" the woman asked softly, as if not wanting to be heard. "I don't see them at church this morning."

Leah's mouth fell open. "I'm sorry, ma'am," she stammered. "George Jolly passed away over a year ago and Polly passed…" Leah swallowed, her mouth suddenly dry. "Just yesterday."

The woman's face instantly lost all color, and if she'd been standing, Leah was certain she would have fainted.

"Miss Barton?"

Leah turned to see Reverend Moore standing in the aisle.

"Yes?" she said politely, though she was more anxious to continue her conversation with the mysterious woman.

"I thought you might wish to say something for Jolly's service after the sermon today."

Leah's heart jumped in trepidation. She did not like to speak in front of people and usually preferred to be unnoticed altogether, but she owed it to Jolly to say something on her behalf. "Of course," she answered.

"Thank you," Jeremiah said with a soft smile. "I—"

"Miss Barton, I'm glad to see you here," Mrs. Beagle interrupted suddenly, as if it wasn't every Sunday that Leah attended church. Twisting around in her seat, she addressed Leah with the same tone as she always used. Though her words were kind, they carried a sharp bite, and none of the façade of kindness managed to reach her eyes.

"I was just telling Mr. Beagle how we needed to give you some turnips," she continued. "Mrs. Pope gave me some that she didn't want. I believe she got them from her son, when he didn't want them. I haven't had turnips in ages. We don't particularly care for them ourselves. But I told Mr. Beagle that there are those in our community who can't afford to be picky, and they would be quite thankful for a bunch of turnips. And I thought of you, of course. I don't imagine the children would care for them, but you wouldn't have to give them a choice. And if that's all you have to eat, then you could be grateful for them and the kindness of others in giving out of their own bounty."

Leah blinked, unsure how to respond. She was pretty sure Mrs. Beagle had just insulted her and disguised it as charity. With her "generous gift," she had just attempted to announce to the reverend, the fine lady beside her, and anyone else who would listen that Leah was a charity case who couldn't turn down turnips and should therefore not be considered acceptable in the higher ranks of society. And by the shrewd light to her eyes, Leah was fairly certain that it was intentional. As usual, Winifred Beagle knew exactly what she was doing.

Thankfully, Leah's mother had taught her how to be a lady, and she refused to join in the silly game of veiled insults. Though she felt a telltale blush, Leah kept her head high, managing a simple, "Thank you, Mrs. Beagle."

"If you will excuse me, I must get the service started," Reverend Moore said with tight lips.

By Jeremiah's stiff gait up front, Leah suspected that he had seen through Mrs. Beagle's charity as well, and was not one bit happy about it.

However, Leah really did have to admire him. He managed to lead the hymns and deliver a fine sermon as if nothing was bothering him, though she suspected a few pointed glances the Beagles' direction during his discourse on loving one another.

Leah wished she could see the face of the woman in front of her. After her announcement about the Jollys, the woman had faced forward and not turned back around once. Leah wanted to ask her if and how she knew the Jollys, but waited until Jeremiah was wrapping up his sermon.

"As many of you know," he said. "We lost a dear member of our town yesterday. Polly Jolly went to receive a great reward in heaven. I find it very appropriate that the sermon today included kindness to others, as unto the Lord. I don't know that there was anyone in Secret better at that than Jolly. We will be taking a brief respite for those who wish to get a drink of water or stretch your legs. Then we will continue with a funeral service for Jolly and end with a graveside service outside."

Not willing to wait a second longer, Leah tapped the woman in front of her on the shoulder lightly and whispered, "Excuse me. Did you know the Jollys?"

But the woman never had a chance to turn, let alone respond.

"Reverend Moore," Mrs. Beagle said loudly, standing to her feet. "If I may, on behalf of the congregation, I would like to make an announcement."

Without waiting for his approval, she marched up to the front. Her face wreathed in a triumphant smile of pride, she spoke, "The members of the congregation have a gift we've been working on, to show our appreciation for our wonderful reverend. We look forward to many years of seeing you in our pulpit. To that end, we felt it appropriate to undertake seeking a bride to be a suitable pastor's wife. We placed advertisements, reviewed applicants, and I am so glad to announce, we selected one. Reverend Moore, I would like to introduce you to Begonia Hardesty, your bride!"

The gasp was audible.

All eyes turned toward the woman hesitantly standing, right in front of Leah.

She wasn't the Beagles' daughter. She was Jeremiah's bride!

Leah's gaze swung to Jeremiah. He positively looked green, as if he would be ill right there in the pulpit at any moment.

Leah felt a tug at her elbow and looked down to see Hazel. With eyes bright, she whispered, "The preacher is getting married!"

Johnny and Curtis were elbowing each other excitedly. And unfortunately, since all the air in the room was sucked out at the unexpected announcement, the only sound was the voices of the two boys who didn't mind the silence at all.

"She's a looker!"

"Do you think he'll give her a big kiss?"

"Shhh," Leah urged, making a grab across Hazel for Johnny, who scooted out of her reach and continued his conversation with his brother.

"Winifred, this isn't right!" Mr. Tuft said, finding his voice as he stood to his feet in dismay. "We agreed—"

"We agreed to order a bride," Mrs. Beagle said curtly. "I was funding the project, so I made the decision. I informed you about the plan. I am not responsible if you didn't understand that."

"But—"

"We made it!" Frankie Smithers barreled into the church, drawing all eyes to the commotion. "I didn't know if we'd make it before everyone left, but we did!"

As he bustled up the aisle, Leah saw that he wasn't alone. A plain-dressed woman was in tow.

Before Leah's mind had a chance to catch up, Frankie was pushing the woman forward.

"Reverend Moore, meet your new wife," he said proudly, his delighted grin stretching from one ear to the other. "Her name be Amy Cox."

Once again, the congregation gasped in shock.

"The preacher is gonna marry two gals!" Curtis screeched in delight.

"No, he ain't!" Johnny said importantly. "He's gotta pick one."

"Well, the first one is purtier than the second," Curtis said thoughtfully.

Leah picked Hazel up and moved the little girl out of the way. Latching onto Johnny's arm, she pushed herself in between the two boys so they could no longer converse.

Fortunately, the shock in the room was so great that nobody else paid any heed to the boys or their commentary.

"How dare you!" Mrs. Beagle spat. "We had an agreement!"

"An agreement which you apparently failed to honor," Mr. Tuft provided. But instead of shock and anger, his voice now held amusement.

Mrs. Beagle flinched at the verbal blow. Recovering quickly, she stood up to her full, rather unimpressive, height. "You knew about this!"

"No, I did not," Mr. Tuft said with dignity. "But I am obviously the only one. The last I heard, we would be reconvening to make the decision in a month. I did not realize both of you would go behind the other's backs within that month!"

"It was my decision to make!" Mrs. Beagle insisted, peering down her nose disdainfully. "Miss Hardesty was the best candidate."

Frankie shuffled his feet nervously. His tone contrite, he spoke, "I 'pologize for not including you, Tuft. A bunch of us knew Mrs. Beagle would never allow what was best for Revered Moore because it wasn't her idea. And we were a bit feared that you wouldn't approve of us just gettin' the job done. We didn't figure to wait for permission. I made a quick run down to Frisco to pick Miss Cox up."

Frankie turned to Jeremiah. "So here she is, Preacher. Ain't she purty?"

"Well, Mr. Smithers, you can make a 'quick trip' back down the mountain and take this woman back where you found her," Mrs Beagle snapped, clearly outraged. "Reverend Moore is already engaged to marry Miss Hardesty."

"He won't be marrying your fancy bit of fluff!" Frankie objected. "He's gonna marry a California girl who knows how to be a good preacher's wife!"

Grunts and nods of agreement greeted Frankie's statement. And some of those supporters were becoming more vocal by the second.

Mr. Tuft raised his hands and his voice. "Now simmer down, everyone! I reckon Reverend Moore would like to have a say in the matter."

All eyes turned to the pastor, who still looked wide-eyed and frozen in complete shock. Never had Leah seen him so off-balance or speechless.

"Excuse me," Begonia Hardesty spoke up from where she stood, still in front of Leah's pew. "Am I to understand that Reverend Moore did not send for me? That he didn't know I was coming until just now?"

"We wished you to be a surprise gift," Mrs. Beagle clarified. "We knew what kind of woman would make for a good match for Secret. We thought to handle all the details, both financial and otherwise, so as not to be a burden on our good pastor."

"You thought wrong," Jeremiah gritted out. And from the look on his face, it seemed as if the shock had finally given way. To anger.

Mrs. Beagle sniffed. "How were we supposed to know that members of our very own congregation would be so deceitful as to go behind our backs!"

Miss Hardesty put her hands on her hips. "Well, you'd better figure it out because I am *not* going back East!"

Up at the front of the room, Amy Cox stood crying softly into a delicate white handkerchief.

Caught up in the drama, Leah barely noticed her brothers wagering on which women they each thought the pastor would choose, not seeming to mind that Leah still stood between them.

Once again, all eyes turned to Jeremiah. The idea flitted through Leah's head that this was his Solomon moment. Everyone turned to him for a wise decision in a dispute involving two women. How he responded would determine their fates, but also leave an indelible mark on his ministry. Leah looked at him anxiously. He had every right to be furious. Could he manage to set that anger aside to make a wise decision?

A loud screech announced the opening of the door once again.

The congregations swung around, and the collective gasp that greeted the newcomer was the loudest yet.

"The preacher's got another gal!" Johnny squealed.

A woman stood in the doorway, dressed in brightly-colored silks and lace. Plumes of feathers waved from an elaborate headpiece. Though her clothes weren't necessarily immodest, their style clearly announced that she hailed from a saloon. However, in this case, Penny Amberly not only worked at the saloon, she owned it.

"Are you gonna marry the preacher too?" Curtis asked with wide eyes.

A smile quirked about Penny Amberly's mouth. Whereas Leah would be humiliated at such an entrance, Mrs. Amberly seemed to almost enjoy the attention.

"Not today," Penny answered, then, turning serious, she scanned the faces of those gathered, finally settling on one.

"Miss Barton," she called, her voice echoing in the hushed sanctuary. "I need you to come with me. Your pa is causing a ruckus down at the saloon."

Panic and embarrassment rivaled for attention, and the panic won. Leah grabbed the hands of Hazel and Curtis and moved to the door, anxious to escape as quickly as possible.

Mrs. Tuft stepped forward. "Leah, you go see to your pa. Let the children stay with me. The Golden Trough is no place for them."

"Thank you," Leah said in relief, transferring Hazel's hand to the other woman's.

With face blazing, Leah hurried to follow Mrs. Amberly. At the door, she chanced one last glance over her shoulder. Everyone was frozen, as if in tableau, all watching her dramatic exit from their positions at the front of the sanctuary. Not only was Leah humiliated and panicked, she was also leaving Frankie and Mrs. Beagle to their battle, Mr. Tuft to his efforts as mediator, and Jeremiah to his two brides.

And possibly the worst part about the whole situation was that she didn't know how it would end.

Chapter 9

"The sheriff will haul Bart to jail if we don't stop him!" Mrs. Amberly said as Leah hurried along beside her. "He's carrying on somethin' fierce, and he won't listen to a word I say. If he hurts someone or breaks something, then I can't help him. He'll be carted off to jail and have to pay for what he broke."

Leah choked back the panic and tried to make her feet move faster. They had no money to pay for property damage!

"What happened?" she asked. "Pa isn't usually the trouble-making kind." Jim Barton, or "Bart," as everyone called him, was generally a happy drunk. Leah suspected drinking was her father's way of not dealing with his grief. Every night, he got to escape through alcohol. But in the past two years, he had never been thrown in jail or become angry to the point of causing harm. Even when he had lost their house, he hadn't been angry.

Defeated, but not mad. To most people, "Bad Bart" was the subject of amusement.

Mrs. Amberly gave a curt shake to her head. "I don't rightly know. He was playing cards with a few slick gamblers who are passing through town. All of a sudden, he got very upset and started shouting. Bart has gambled before, but I've never seen him upset, even when he lost. I left Gus to watch things and ran over to get you."

"Thank you," Leah said, appreciating that, contrary to Mrs. Amberly's soiled reputation, Leah's experience with the saloon owner had always involved the older woman being kind and considerate. "But I don't know that he'll listen to me if he won't listen to you."

"Mrs. Amberly shook her head and pursed her lips together. "I don't know where he got the money to gamble. I haven't paid him more than his tab in quite some time."

Instant anger sparked deep inside Leah, taking her breath away. She had often wondered how her father always managed to have money for his alcohol. He would occasionally find money she had hidden for food, but it was never enough to do the regular nightly drinking her father enjoyed. She had long suspected he did work for Penny and Gus Amberly. She'd even seen him unloading crates into the saloon. But to hear Mrs. Amberly so casually mention that she supplied her father with the poison that was ruining his life, was more than Leah could take.

Leah stopped ten feet from the saloon doors, as if she'd hit a wall. "Mrs. Amberly, you may have to forgive me for saying so, but don't you find it wrong to pay for a man to get drunk every night while his children are left to fend for themselves?"

Mrs. Amberly's eyes flashed, not with equal anger, but with compassion. "Yes, I do think it wrong, Leah," she responded quietly. "But I think it more wrong if your father stole the money you earned for food and rent, in order to spend it on his drink."

Leah blinked. Was Mrs. Amberly really trying to protect them?

Quietly, but with determination, Mrs. Amberly continued. "As you know, my husband was injured and is unable to walk or do much of what is necessary to keep the saloon. I employ your father to do much of the lifting and labor that is difficult for me. In return, I pay for his drink. Not enough that he passes out, but enough so that he doesn't take money from you to fuel his thirst. I don't pretend to be a moral woman, Leah. If it was in my power, I would ensure that your father never drank another drop. But that is not my decision, it is his. Until then, I do what I can."

Leah struggled to find words. She had blamed this woman and thought awful things of her. Now she realized Mrs. Amberly had only been trying to help in a situation that was in no way her responsibility.

"I'm so sorry, Mrs. Amberly," Leah said humbly.

Mrs. Amberly waved her hand dismissively. "Call me Penny. You had every right to be angry. It certainly appeared that I was every bit as evil as everyone thinks."

At the sound of a loud shout, the women abandoned their conversation and hurried through the swinging bar doors. Leah was so anxious to find her father that she forgot her trepidation, and was inside the saloon before she realized she'd just entered what many in the church congregation would view as a "den of sin."

Her eyes quickly adjusting to the dim light, she gasped at the sight of her father, shouting and hefting a bar chair above his head as he aimed at the dandy-dressed man beside him.

"Pa, no!" Leah shrieked, rushing over and immediately attaching herself to her father's elbow.

"Bart, I insist on you telling me what is going on!" Penny said, sliding herself between Bart and his nemesis.

Paying no heed to Leah, Bart shouted, "This man's a cheat!"

The gambler smirked. "He lost a bet, and now he's a sore loser."

Leah felt her eyes grow wide. What did he bet? He had nothing of value! And Penny had just said she hadn't given him any money.

Perhaps even more troubling was the realization that her pa hadn't been this upset when he had lost their house and claim in an apparent bet gone bad.

Tossing aside the chair, Bart lunged for the other man, making it past Penny to grab his arm.

The man back-pedaled, trying to get away from Bart, but Bart held him fast. Rearing back his fist, Bart swung for the gambler's nose. But the gambler ducked at the last minute, causing Bart to only knock off his hat.

The momentum carrying him forward, Bart lost his balance and careened into a table.

Bart picked himself up, once again grabbing a wooden chair and raising it high above his head. This time, the gambler was caught between the table and a stack of over-turned chairs and had no way to escape. Bart's eyes flashed wild as he raised the chair to a horrifying peak, ready to bring it down hard on the other man's head.

"Pa, please!" Leah begged, grabbing his arm and pulling at it with her full weight.

But he didn't seem to hear

Her efforts seemed only that of an annoying insect.

"Pa, stop this instant!" Leah shrieked. "Ma would be so ashamed of you!"

He paused. The chair still wobbled at its crest, but the tension was gone.

With the sobering light of sanity returning in his gaze, Bart brought the chair down, setting it to the floor with a gentle touch.

"What did you bet, Pa?" Leah asked, her dry, cracking voice echoing in the sudden silence of the saloon.

Bowing his head in shame, Bart wouldn't look at her.

"Bart, just pay the man and be done with it," Penny urged. "He isn't worth being thrown in jail. You've been here all night and half the day. It's time to go home."

"Chickens," the gambler said with a sneer. "He owes me a nice flock of chickens."

"Chickens?" Leah choked. "*My* chickens?"

Though Bart still wouldn't look at his daughter, the miserable look of guilt said enough.

Penny's eyes lit with understanding. Turning to the gambler, she spoke up quickly. "I'm sorry, sir, but it seems like you're the victim of a bad bet. Bart doesn't own any chickens to offer in a bet."

"Sure he does!" the man cackled. "If she's his daughter, then both she and her chickens belong to him!"

As sickening as it seemed, he was right. Leah was under her father's roof. It wouldn't matter that she paid the rent and had purchased the chickens herself with her own wages. Everyone saw it as a man's world, where a woman couldn't seem to own anything, even chickens.

There was no way out.

"Now, wait!" Penny objected. "Don't take the girl's chickens. I'll pay you what they're worth, and Bart can owe me."

The man's face scrunched up, as if he was actually considering the offer.

Not waiting for his answer, Penny bustled over to the long bar to retrieve the funds.

"I don't think so," the gambler said, halting her with his voice and a crafty grin. "The bet was for chickens, and I aim to have chickens."

Leah closed her eyes and focused on breathing. Though she appreciated Penny's offer, this man wasn't going to be satisfied unless he was able to fully enjoy the pain he was inflicting.

"I'll have them ready for you in the morning," Leah offered quietly, completely defeated.

"No." The gambler raised an eyebrow as if daring her to challenge him. "I'll take those chickens right now. I'm in the mood for some fried chicken for supper."

Leah struggled to breathe. "But they're laying hens!"

He shrugged his suit-clad shoulders. "They're chickens. They aren't going to live through the winter here in the mountains. I better put them to good use before then. How many chickens are there? Maybe the cook at the hotel will be interested in a bit of extra money to fry all of them up right for my friends here at the saloon.

By the sound of grunting and the sight of men literally licking their lips, Leah knew she wouldn't get any help from the rowdy bunch of miners who likely hadn't tasted fried chicken in a month of Sundays.

Though unable to speak, Leah nodded, her chin trembling. Tugging on her father's elbow, she turned to the swinging saloon doors. She paused right before them, waiting while Bart shrugged on his threadbare coat.

Hearing voices, she peeked above the door, seeing that the church congregation had dismissed and was dispersing through the streets of Secret.

Leah's stomach turned. If it wasn't bad enough that her father had gambled away her means of putting food on their table, now she had to live her humiliation publicly. There was no way around walking out of the saloon alongside a gambler and her drunkard father, right in front of the Sunday morning church congregation.

Before she had mentally prepared herself, the men lurched through the doors, and she followed in their wake. Her eyes lit on Mrs. Tuft trying to herd her sister and two brothers down the street.

Leah hurried to them, hoping to retrieve her siblings and make a hasty exit before the entire saloon saga made the rounds of open-mouthed onlookers.

"Thank you for watching the children, Mrs. Tuft," Leah said. "I'm sorry to have missed Jolly's service."

"Oh, you didn't miss it," Miss Tuft assured. "Reverend Moore rescheduled it for tomorrow. Given the circumstances, he didn't feel it appropriate to conduct a funeral today."

Leah felt an insistent tug on her dress. She looked down to find a bright-eyed Curtis. "I was right! Preacher *is* going to marry both of them!"

"No, he ain't," Johnny scoffed. "He's just gonna court both of them, but then he can only choose one!"

"I believe you both are mistaken," Mrs. Tuft said in her most proper tone. "Revered Moore said he would interview each woman and spend the week in prayer. Next Sunday he will announce the decision he has made."

"So he will marry one of them," Leah surmised, feeling the shadow of despair crowd close.

"Not necessarily," Mrs. Tuft hedged. "He was not happy about being placed in this difficult situation. I believe his decision had as much to do with the congregation's actions and what to do about two women who both feel very misled. While he prays and talks with the women, each group is responsible to provide for the accommodations of their bride in the hotel for the week." She shook her head sadly. "He was very clear about his disapproval and disappointment in the actions of his congregation."

A strident voice caught their attention and both women looked up to see Mrs. Beagle still arguing angrily as she moved down the street.

Mrs. Tuft sighed. "Unfortunately, some of us aren't quite ready to see the shame in the situation and accept responsibility for it."

In the distance, having apparently escorted his two brides to the hotel, Leah saw Jeremiah exit the building, his head bowed low.

Leah gulped and turned away, bracing herself to try not to feel the sting. After all, she deserved some of the blame as well. She could have told the reverend and stopped the entire mess from ever happening.

Looking around, she realized that her father and the gambler weren't waiting for her. Instead, the gambler had already procured a wagon and the two men were already well down the street, headed to collect her chickens. If she didn't hurry, her father would not wait for her to pay his debt. The chickens would be gone before she got there.

"Excuse me, Mrs. Tuft," Leah said hurriedly. "I must go ready my chickens for their new owner."

"New owner?" the woman asked in confusion. Then, looking from Leah to the men in the distance, understanding dawned. "Oh no, Leah!"

"What's wrong?" Jeremiah asked, arriving at the scene.

Leah, couldn't answer or even manage to look at Jeremiah.

Ducking Mrs. Tuft's look of pity, she pulled Hazel to her hip, grabbed Curtis's hand and hurried away, hoping Johnny would take the cue and follow while Mrs. Tuft explained the situation to Jeremiah.

Hazel bounced against her, and her legs burned with the effort of her footsteps hastening her home.

Leah tried not to think. Tried not to feel. One part of her wanted to believe that God would care for them, that the Bible was true and that not even a sparrow could fall without His knowing. But the other part of her was consumed in fear. Those chickens were so much more than chickens.

And when she tenderly packed the protesting hens in a box, she fully understood that her father hadn't just gambled away some birds. Long after the wagon had rolled away, Leah stood watching, knowing that all hope had just left in a box full of chickens.

Chapter 10

Leah rolled over and pulled the quilt over her head. She wished she didn't have to get up today. There was no scratching of chickens in the coop to greet her. No eggs to gather. No money to collect on her egg delivery.

A chair scraped across the floor, and Leah bolted up in bed at the unfamiliar sound. Her father sat at the table, staring at the dwindling flames in the fireplace.

Leah had fully expected him to take off last night. After the incident with the gambler, Bart would have more need than usual to drown his sorrows. But he hadn't. Leah had made dinner, and he stayed. Not speaking a word, he ate every bite of his beans and then disappeared into the bedroom.

Seeing him here, calmly awaiting the arrival of morning and appearing completely sober, was unprecedented in the last two years.

Carefully, so as not to disturb Hazel sleeping peacefully beside her on the pine bough mattress, Leah extracted herself from the bed. Wrapping an extra quilt around herself, Leah stood and went to put another log on the fire.

"I'll have breakfast ready in a few minutes," she announced to her father. She quickly began to gather what few supplies she still had. She may be able to cook up the couple of eggs she had left and make some johnnycakes to go with them.

After a few moments of silence, Bart spoke, the sound of his gruff voice causing Leah to jump. "I'm sorry about the chickens, daughter."

Her father rarely spoke to her. The few times he did, his words had no true meaning, keeping mostly to remarks on the weather when he was sober and drunken nonsense when he wasn't. That he spoke to her directly, and that it was an actual apology with no excuses, was something that Leah didn't know how to respond to. It had never happened.

Should she say that it was okay? But it wasn't. Those chickens were important to Leah and their livelihood. And they hadn't been his to gamble away.

Should she get angry and lecture him on his behavior? Or on all of his responsibilities that Leah had to handle? Or on his drunkenness and sin that was victimizing his family?

It wouldn't do any good. She was his daughter, and as such, no matter what he did, it was not her place to reprimand and disrespect him.

All she could do was attempt to make sure her own conscience was clear. "I appreciate you saying that, Pa. But you may have to give me a little time. I will forgive you, but it might take me a while to feel that forgiveness."

She wished she could be more righteous and forgive him right now. But she couldn't. Her only hope was that God would grant her a little patience on the forgiveness part and a little credit for her honesty.

Bart had started some coffee brewing on the fire. Leah now took the kettle down and checked to make sure it was ready.

Bart watched her while she worked. Though she didn't look at him, she could feel his gaze following her.

"You were right," he finally said roughly. "Your ma would be mighty ashamed of me, and rightly so. I wish I could tell you I'd do better. To promise that it wouldn't happen again. But, truthfully, if you buy more chickens, I may do the same thing." Bart shook his head sadly. "I am not a good man, and there's no use pretending to be. What they say about me is true. I really am 'Bad Bart.'"

"Yes, you are," Leah affirmed simply, without a trace of sympathy. Her father didn't need or deserve meaningless platitudes to make himself feel better, and he certainly wouldn't get them from her.

"But," she said thoughtfully, pouring the brewed coffee into two chipped mugs. "I suppose if people weren't bad, they wouldn't need God. Someone who was truly good would have no need of a savior. And if we could truly be good without God, then He would have no need to send Jesus."

"It's too late for me, daughter. Not even God could change me. After your ma died, I tried to talk to God, and it just didn't take. I guess there was just too much bad in me. If I tried now, I'd just disappoint Him as I do everyone else."

Leah set a mug on the rough table in front of her father. "Just because we ask God to save us, doesn't mean we are automatically good. I don't think that's how it works. It's hard. Sometimes you will still want to do bad things, maybe all the time. But I think God must help us to be good. Maybe he makes us want good things more than the bad. Maybe God can make you want to please Him and take care of your family more than you want to drink."

Bart shook his head, his expression firmly desolate. "It's too hard. I'll fail."

"Probably," Leah said with a shrug. "But you've really got nothing to lose. We certainly have nothing left for you to gamble away."

"It's too late for me. I've been the same for so long, it'd be useless to try to be different. Like tryin' to put nice clean clothes on a body that's already filthy with dirt. I was never a saint, even before your ma passed. People will only ever see me as Bad Bart. Why should I even bother to try?"

"Because it's the right thing to do," Leah said simply. "Because God means for you to be something more than the town drunk." Though she'd started out just talking casually about what she felt and believed, the more she spoke, the more fervent she became. Not because she wanted her pa to change, but because she wanted him to understand that God had so much more for him than what he could find at the bottom of a bottle.

"God's purpose isn't dependent on others' opinions," she continued earnestly. "The only opinion that matters is His. I think if you ask Him to, He'll do the work to make you into someone who pleases Him."

"'For it is God which worketh in you both to will and to of his good pleasure.' That's somewhere in Philippians, ain't it?"

Leah's mouth fell open in shock. "Philippians 2:13."

Bart nodded. "Thought so." Seeing the look on her face, he bristled. "Don't look at me that way. I'm not a complete heathen. I sometimes listened when your ma spoke about the Bible."

Leah nodded. "Philippians was her favorite. She had the whole book memorized. I just didn't know that you'd listened."

Bart nodded. "Well, it was rather hard not to when she recited that thing whenever she did laundry."

"And when she was cooking," Leah offered.

"And when she was outside working," Bart remembered.

"And before bed," Leah supplied.

"And a few times I woke up to hear her reciting it in her sleep!" Bart laughed.

Leah laughed with him. Though their laughter sounded almost foreign, even to her own ears, it felt so good. Leah didn't remember the last time she had laughed, especially with her pa.

"Is breakfast ready yet?" a sleepy voice asked from a pine bough mattress in the corner.

"In just a few minutes," Leah told Johnny as she hurried back to her duties of pouring the batter into the pan for johnnycakes. "I need to hurry," Leah said, realizing that time was slipping away from her. "I have to get all the chores done before Jolly's service. Since it's supposed to be before lunch, I don't have a lot of time."

"I don't think I'm up to Jolly's funeral," Bart said. "She was a good woman. A good friend to your ma."

With a quick glance at his face, Leah saw all trace of laughter gone. In fact, he looked quite stricken.

Then Leah understood. Was this the reason her father had gone on such a drinking and gambling binge? Jolly's death had probably brought back the death of Leah's ma.

Leah sighed and turned to her work. Now, seeing the grief clearly etched in lines on his face, Leah wouldn't be at all surprised if he took off again this evening on another binge, despite any good conversation they'd just had.

She couldn't make her father turn his life around, and she couldn't make the pain get better for him. All she could do was pray and put one foot in front of the other. She would carry on, trying not to let her life depend on her pa in any way.

The rest of the morning passed in a blur. Leah barely had time to think, which was good. She got the boys up and off to school, and she and Hazel even made it to the church on time for Jolly's service. When Jeremiah called her to the front, she managed to speak about Jolly, telling of her wonderful friend, without bursting into tears.

After the memorial inside, there was a short graveside service. Even though Jolly had already been buried, mourners gathered in the little cemetery while Reverend Moore said a prayer and spoke a few more words of comfort. Leah saw a man standing in the shadows of a tree, watching the proceedings. From a distance, he looked a lot like her father, but she couldn't be sure. After the service, she turned to find him and get a better look, but the man was already gone.

Since it was a Monday, Leah didn't have time to linger at the graveside. Mondays meant she had to clean both the church and the mercantile. Leaving Hazel in the care of Mrs. Pope, Leah skipped lunch in order to make it through her cleaning duties at the mercantile and make it back shortly after Johnny and Curtis arrived home from school.

Tired and hungry, Leah managed to finish her work according to plan and hurried home. Walking up to the house, Leah saw the two boys busy with their hole.

"Have you boys seen Pa?" Leah asked, though she was not in the least optimistic.

"Nope!" Johnny answered without even pausing his shovel.

Leah was not in the least surprised. Bart was probably already at the saloon, maybe doing work for Penny in order to pay for his nightly beverage. She hadn't expected anything different, but maybe something she said would bounce around in his head and one day make a difference. He had remembered that verse in Philippians, so maybe her words wouldn't be entirely wasted breath.

"I'm grabbing something to eat, and then I will take you boys to Mrs. Pope's house while I clean the church. I want to be done before supper." With the temperature dropping lower with the setting sun, Leah didn't want to be out long after dark.

"Aw, do we have to?" Johnny whined. "Mrs. Pope isn't any fun at all!"

"Yes, you have to," Leah said dryly, leaving them to their "work," and walking to the front door.

But right in front of the door, blocking her from entering, sat a plump, brown chicken.

Suddenly aware of familiar clucking noises, Leah turned a full circle, now noticing multiple chickens pecking around the front of the house. But they weren't just any chickens.

They were *her* chickens.

"Chickens!" Leah said, forcing the word past her tight throat. "How... ? Why... ? My chickens!"

"Oh, we forgot to tell you," Curtis said, as if remembering that the grass was green. "Preacher brought them by."

"Reverend Moore?" Leah asked, completely dumbfounded. "How did he get my chickens?"

"Don't know," Johnny said with a shrug. "He said to tell you that they are a present from Jolly."

"But that don't make sense," Curtis said, his brow furrowing in confusion. "How could Jolly give Leah chickens from heaven?"

This actually made Johnny pause. His chin rested on the handle of the shovel as he thought. "Wasn't there somewhere in the Bible where God sent birds to the Israelites in the desert? Maybe it's something like that."

Curtis's eyes grew big. "If they really are chickens from heaven, what do you think their eggs taste like? Do you think Leah can get more money for heavenly eggs than for regular ones?"

Leah stifled her giggle, deciding there was no use in trying to talk sense into her brothers. She gently picked the doorway hen up, giving her a few loving pats before moving her out of the way.

With a smile, her eyes swept over her chickens once more before stepping into the house. She had fully expected her little flock to all be fried by now, but instead, a quick count revealed every single one to be present and accounted for.

Though she doubted Johnny and Curtis's theory, she didn't doubt that her chickens were heavenly birds. God had somehow arranged to miraculously give them back to her.

The how part is what would require a little more investigation.

Chapter 11

Leah's feet dragged their way down the church steps.

She was weary. After everything that had happened with Jolly, the bride fiasco, and then with her pa, her emotions couldn't handle anything more. Added to that, she'd just cleaned the entire church in record time, and her body was sore and protesting.

It was twilight. Things at the church hadn't gone as quickly as she would have liked, but at least she should be able to collect the children and make it home soon after dark.

Leah trudged down the path through the graveyard, trying to think of what she had at home to feed the children.

Seeing movement, she froze.

A figure was behind a tree at the edge of the graveyard, He seemed to be spying on a wagon on the road directly below.

The figure moved slightly, and Leah's breath caught.

It was Johnny!

She didn't *think* it was Johnny, she *knew* it was!

Without hesitation, she marched across the graveyard to the tree and pulled the boy to his feet.

"Johnny Barton, what on earth are you doing?" But she knew what he was doing. "Who are you spying on?" she asked instead.

Then she saw.

Immediately letting Johnny go, she flung herself behind the tree, crouching right beside her brother.

Jeremiah Moore and Begonia Hardesty sat in the wagon below.

"I was just watching!" Johnny insisted.

"Why?" Leah hissed. "Reverend Moore deserves some privacy!"

The irony of her statement wasn't completely lost on her. At that very instant, she was hiding just as Johnny was, and she would very much like to know what was being said in the wagon below.

"They're just talking. And I can't hear anything," Johnny said, as if offended that all of his efforts weren't compromising the pastor's privacy after all. "Pastor talked to the other lady earlier. And I watched that too. But I couldn't hear anything. She cried though. I thought for sure he'd kiss her when she cried. But he didn't." Johnny sighed. "I really wanted him to kiss her. That would have been somethin' to see."

"So nothing has happened?" Leah asked hesitantly. She really shouldn't be doing this. She'd already learned her lesson about spying and eavesdropping. However, at this point, there was no way to drag Johnny out from behind the tree without getting the attention of Jeremiah and Miss Hardesty. Then they would realize they'd been spied on and would most likely assume that Leah had been watching as well.

"No, it's been boring," Johnny said, thoroughly disgusted. "I thought a pastor courtin' two gals would be a good show, but it ain't. They just talk. What's the fun in that?" The boy sprawled out on the leaves as if tired of it all, but still wanting to have the best view.

Leah felt relieved, even though she didn't understand why. It wasn't any of her business if Reverend Moore really did court both women, or even if he kissed them! But for some reason, the scene below was very important to her.

It all looked very formal with Jeremiah dressed in his suit and Miss Hardesty, in her fancy navy blue frock with matching cloak, sitting on the seat beside him. They didn't sit overly close. Their heads weren't even inclined toward each other. There was nothing improper, or even dramatic, about it. And yet, Leah watched their every breath with pounding heart.

Leah was completely still for the space of several minutes, straining to hear their voices, but she still couldn't understand a single word.

"Stop wriggling, Johnny!" she whispered fiercely. Every time the boy moved, the dry leaves crackled, and Leah was sure if he would just be still, she could hear better.

Johnny wriggled some more.

Reverend Moore reached his hand back and rubbed his neck.

Johnny wriggled.

Miss Hardesty reached up to right her hat, as if the wind had knocked it slightly askew.

But there was no wind.

Johnny wriggled.

"Ow!"

The cry was loud enough to hear. Leah's eyes flew wide as she saw Jeremiah rub at his face, almost as if he'd been hit.

As if following an invisible line, her gaze traced from Jeremiah's cheek, all the way back to the slingshot in Johnny's hands as he lay on his belly beside her.

"Johnny!" she shrieked, pulling him to his feet once again. "What are you doing!"

"I'm just having a little fun!" he protested.

Leah looked down to see a pile of walnuts where he'd lain. By the look of things, she was sure that his entertainment hadn't just begun.

"You weren't 'just watching'!" she accused. "And you definitely weren't bored!"

Without allowing time to talk herself out of it, she entwined her arm with his and pulled him down the little hill.

Leah was out of breath when they reached the wagon, but she didn't wait. She bravely looked up at Jeremiah and Miss Hardesty, not allowing her gaze to waver. "My brother, Johnny, has something to say to you."

"Johnny?" she asked pointedly, nudging him in the back.

"I'm sorry," he mumbled with his head down.

"Johnny, speak up so they can hear you," Leah instructed. "And say what you're apologizing for."

Raising his head, Johnny spoke clearly, "I'm sorry for spying on you and using my slingshot to hit you with walnuts."

Leah nodded. "If either of you have any chores or work to do, I would very much like Johnny to help you as part of his penance."

Reverend Moore and Miss Hardesty looked at each other with raised eyebrows.

"I may have an idea of something Mr. Johnny could assist me with right now," Miss Hardesty said with a smile. "I am dining with the Beagles this evening, and Winifred asked if I would stop at the mercantile and see if a package had arrived in the mail today. She didn't have a chance to check earlier. But since I don't know how large the package is, I might need a strong lad to assist me in carrying it."

Leah understood that Miss Hardesty was simply trying to be nice. She didn't really require help, but was offering a simple way for Johnny to complete his punishment. Though it wasn't the type of consequence Leah felt he deserved, she would make do with what she got.

With a stern, deliberate look Johnny's direction, Leah waited for him to offer his services.

"Well, I could probably do that," he said reluctantly. "But then I have to get back right away. I don't want to be late for Mrs. Tuft's dinner."

"Mrs. Tuft's dinner?" Leah sputtered. "I left you with Mrs. Pope! Why is Mrs. Tuft serving you dinner?"

"Mrs. Pope wasn't feeling too well, so Mrs. Tuft took us to her house. She's ever so much nicer than Mrs. Pope anyway. And she said if we did a good job of eating our dinner, she would let us choose a sweet treat from the mercantile!"

"You should have plenty of time," Miss Hardesty assured. "I understand that Mr. Tuft closes the mercantile around the dinner hour anyway, so we should have just enough time for you to escort me on my errand and then to the Beagles' house."

Leah, not even hearing Miss Hardesty's sensible response, looked at Johnny opened-mouthed. "Oh no! I mustn't let them take advantage of Mrs. Tuft's kindness. She doesn't need to feed them dinner! Excuse me, but I need to go collect the children."

"Miss Barton, wait!" Jeremiah called, stopping her before she'd taken two steps. "If I may have a word with you, I don't think there's any harm in waiting. Besides, it will take a few minutes for young Johnny to complete his chore for Miss Hardesty."

"Reverend Moore, thank you for the lovely drive, but if you don't mind, I think I'll have this young man escort me from here. I'm sure I won't be able to locate a finer tour guide, and I'd like to stretch my legs in a brisk walk before dinner."

Jeremiah assisted her down from the wagon, and Johnny, developing a bit of a glow at her praise, took her arm and dutifully led her down the street.

Though anxious to be on her way, Leah politely turned to Jeremiah. He must want to tell her about the chickens. And she really wanted to know, but who knew what torture her siblings were putting the proper Mrs. Tuft through!

As if wanting to keep their conversation private, Jeremiah took her arm and led her to the shelter of some tall pines lining the road. Leah looked up and still could see the tree where she and Curtis had hidden, but it was now thankfully empty of eavesdroppers.

Whatever Jeremiah had to say to her, it must be important, which troubled her. Maybe he needed to tell her about something besides the chickens. Was he about to give her bad news?

Jeremiah turned to her, his eyes warm. "Leah, if Mrs. Tuft wants to bestow a little kindness on the children, you should let her. She and Mr. Tuft were never able to have children of their own. If she invited them to her house and is making them dinner, that could be a very good sign. She doesn't form relationships easily, but if she were to bond with any children, I think that could be a wonderful blessing for both them and her."

Leah blinked. "I had no idea," she said. "If it would help her, of course I will share the children as much as she wants." Leah bit her lip, thinking. "I guess I'm just not used to thinking that allowing someone to help could be a blessing to them. I always feel awful about inconveniencing anyone because they help me."

"Don't you remember, Leah, 'It is more blessed to give than to receive?' I think that very much includes giving of yourself, not just things. You seem to enjoy giving to others, right? Did you find it a blessing to leave those treats for Jolly on her doorstep, even though you didn't have a lot extra to share?"

Leah felt a slow smile that began in the depths of her soul. "Why, yes, it was a blessing. I loved doing that."

Jeremiah nodded. "Let others have that same blessing of serving you."

Leah nodded and then smiled shyly. "I really think if others are blessed by serving me, then it has been a twice blessed day. Mrs. Tuft is helping with the children, and you performed a miracle and rescued my chickens."

Jeremiah smiled. "I can't claim the blessing for that good deed. It belongs all to Jolly."

At Leah's look of confusion, Jeremiah explained. "Jolly didn't leave you her claim because she knew your pa would just gamble it away. Instead, she left it to the church. But she also left a healthy amount of money she and her husband had saved. As minister of the church, she entrusted it to me with the provision that it be used to help you whenever the need arose. I felt buying back the chickens was a need Jolly would approve of."

Leah's mind spun in circles. How much money did Jolly leave? Was it all to be spent on her? Did buying the chickens cost all of the money?

"But how did you buy them back?" Leah asked, finally finding a question she deemed appropriate. "The man my pa lost them to wasn't interested in selling them back. Mrs. Amberly tried. He wanted them for fried chicken. In fact, he seemed so set on it that I'm surprised that there were any chickens left, let alone all of them!"

There was just a tinge of pride in the reverend's smile as he explained, "I'm sure it was a combination of quality persuasion on my part and the fact that he really couldn't get any help at all with frying up the chickens. Everyone in town flat refused no matter how much he offered them. They all knew those chickens were yours and wanted no part of him taking them from you. Turns out live chickens are a tad more work than dead ones. After one night of ownership, he was a little more ready to make a deal. I'm sure the fact that I'm a preacher may have also reminded him that his actions may not be in keeping with biblical morality."

As if summarizing everything, he finally looked at Leah again and said, "But I'd like you to believe that it was first and foremost my persuasion skills."

Leah laughed. Though she was amused at his tale, she was also touched that the community had stood up for her. She would not have thought that they cared that much, especially when money was involved. But despite his explanation, Leah still recognized Jeremiah as the hero. "Oh, I do believe it had everything to do with your persuasion skills," she answered glibly. Then her tone turning serious, she added, "I know I wouldn't have gotten them back if not for you. Jolly's money may have paid for them, but not without your efforts. You didn't have to do it. But thank you for doing it anyway."

"Now that I've answered your questions, it's time for you to answer one of mine. I think you took care of Johnny well enough, but what are you planning to do for your penance?"

Leah's breath caught and her eyes involuntarily darted up to the tree by the graveyard.

Jeremiah looked at her knowingly. "I seem to remember seeing more than one head peeking out from behind that tree."

"I… um…" She'd been caught! "I'm sorry. I really didn't intend to spy on you."

"Oh, really?" Jeremiah asked, teasingly. "I was rather hoping you did."

Leah, not understanding at all what he meant, plunged forward with her explanation. "I saw Johnny spying and went over to reprimand him. Then I saw you and Miss Hardesty. I panicked. I'm sorry. I shouldn't have done it. I didn't want to interrupt and thought you would think the worst of me if you saw me up there, so I just hid. And watched. And now you think the worst of me anyway."

"On the contrary, I thought maybe you had a reason for watching. Maybe not a righteous reason, but one that I might appreciate. I don't think I could ever think bad of you, Leah."

"Yes, you can." Leah, suddenly feeling the cold air, buried her hands in the folds of her cloak. But she wasn't sure if the chill was due to the temperature or her own anxiety. "If you don't think bad of me now, I'm sure you will when I tell you the complete truth. You may excuse me from making penance over spying, but when I confess what I've done, you will most certainly agree that I deserve your bad favor and any penance you deem appropriate."

"Why don't you let me be the judge of that?" Jeremiah said easily.

Clearly, he didn't understand the severity of Leah's transgressions.

Leah gulped, and before she had time to over-think what she was saying, she confessed. "I knew about the congregation's plans to order you a bride. I overheard their meeting." Leah winced, realizing she very likely appeared to have an eavesdropping problem. Maybe she really was a snoop! "I wanted to tell you so many times, but I never managed to get it out. I wasn't included in the meeting and they didn't want my help. But I didn't think it was right and thought you should be told. I tried to find out more about their plans." Another wince. "But I got caught eavesdropping and was told, in very certain terms, that I should not interfere or there would be consequences."

"You were threatened," Jeremiah stated, his jaw tense.

Leah shrugged, "I felt they were threats. But that still isn't a good enough excuse. Yes, I was concerned for my family should I tell, but I could have anyway and trusted that God would take care of us. I also could have told before that, when I first heard them making plans. I didn't know if maybe you'd like a mail order bride. It didn't seem right to me, but everyone else seemed to think it was a great idea."

Jeremiah blew out an exasperated breath. Then, seeing the look on Leah's face, he quickly explained. "I'm not upset with you at all, Leah. It wasn't your idea. You didn't participate in any way. You could have told me, but there should have never been the need. And I understand why you didn't. You did try. I remember you wanting to tell me something, but you never got a chance. And I didn't do a good job of following up with you, even though I knew there was something bothering you."

Jeremiah bent, picked up a pinecone, and threw it as hard as he could. "I feel like a complete failure," he admitted tensely. "That's my only explanation as to why my congregation would find it acceptable to order me a mail order bride. And then, to make matters worse, they couldn't agree. So they deceived each other and ended up ordering me two! Along the way, they apparently thought it also acceptable to threaten those who could get in the way of their plan. None of that is in line with biblical principles. Obviously, I'm a very unsuccessful minister if those under my care see such behavior as acceptable."

Leah looked at him in concern. He was blaming himself? "Jeremiah, if you look at it another way, your congregation really likes and appreciates you. They are terrified that you'll leave and were really seeking a way to both please you and keep you in their town. They were misguided, but their hearts were in a right place. I know they have issues, but there was only one person who threatened me. Their actions show just how much they need you and good biblical instruction."

"I can guess who it was that was in charge and made the threats," Jeremiah said dryly. "I will be talking to several members of the congregation, but to her specifically. I pray God will give me the words He would have me speak." Jeremiah acted as if he would say more, but then shook his head. "I'll take care of it. That's all I will say."

Leah nodded. "I'll definitely be praying for you to have wisdom. Besides dealing with the congregation, I really believe that any man with two brides is going to need a lot of wisdom."

Jeremiah startled a little, as if he really couldn't believe she was teasing him.

Leah tried to control her smile, but couldn't. "Curtis really does believe you're going to marry both of them. I think that's why Johnny was trying so hard to spy on you. He wanted to know if his brother was right! But you obviously weren't meeting his expectations, so he found other ways to entertain himself."

Jeremiah laughed, his eyes dancing merrily. "Well, I really do hate disappointing a young lad like that!" He shook his head. "I really am mystified. I don't know what the congregation was thinking. If they really wanted me to get married, I would have thought it much easier to play matchmaker closer to home."

Now it was Leah's turn to be surprised. "There aren't any suitable candidates closer to home. As you know, men vastly outnumber the women in California, and that is especially true in Secret. The closest they could think to find a quality woman was San Francisco. But Mrs. Beagle, of course, thought they would get a better result from back East."

"I'm not sure what you mean." Jeremiah raised his eyebrows. "Am I not talking to a 'suitable candidate' right now?"

Leah's eyes locked with his. She couldn't look away. Her mouth went completely dry, and for the space of several heartbeats, she couldn't remember how to speak.

Finally clearing her throat, she spoke, "I'm not... I can't... Jeremiah, I am not the kind of woman they would want for a pastor's wife. Most of them see me as just a girl anyway. I was never even considered."

"Maybe you should have been."

Jeremiah hadn't been here long enough. But how could she explain?

Leah shivered, but she didn't know if it was more from the moment's intensity and her agonizing thoughts or from the snow that was now lightly falling.

"Jeremiah, you don't understand," Leah managed. "I'm not good enough. My father spends every night at the saloon, and my family is mostly viewed as a charity case. I would never be accepted as a church member, let alone the pastor's wife!"

Jeremiah's head leaned closer to hers. Though the sun was completely gone past the horizon, the falling snow seemed to make everything lighter, adding a soft glow to the trees, ground, and even the air. Through the filmy veil of snowflakes, Jeremiah's eyes sparked with intensity. "Leah, you've said things like that before, but I don't believe them."

"How can you not believe them? Don't you see—"

"Let me show you what I see."

His fingers caressed her cheek, sending a shiver through Leah. But this time, Leah knew she couldn't blame the snow.

Then, his lips were on hers.

Leah's breath caught in surprise, but then the sheer exhilaration kept any breath from returning.

His lips were gentle, yet there was nothing hesitant about the kiss. He was very clearly showing her that all of her arguments were completely irrelevant.

And she wanted to believe him. For the few blissfully wonderful moments when his lips caressed hers, she thought that this beautiful glimpse of paradise might be possible.

Then, slowly, their lips parted.

She breathed. Opening her eyes, she looked up at him, trying to gather her wayward senses.

"Leah, I see you. I see your beauty. And your goodness that reminds me of our Savior. I see your generosity and gentleness. I see your love and dedication for others. I see how hard you work. In circumstances that would make other young women bitter, you shine. Leah, don't let others' opinions dictate who you are meant to be. What matters is how God views you. And from my view, I think you would make any man a wonderful bride, especially a pastor."

Oh, how she wanted to believe him!

Trying to think, her eyes slid shut. Flashing through her mind's eye, she saw others' faces as they looked at her. She read the judgment, the pity, the disdain.

It didn't matter what Jeremiah thought. She would always see the way they looked at her. She would never be good enough.

Leah sought a way to explain it to Jeremiah. How would he understand that the ideal didn't matter? People shouldn't judge others or make them feel inferior. A woman should not be judged on her father's behavior.

Unfortunately, no amount of hoping would change the reality, and the real Secret, California, in 1870 was what they must deal with.

Though she would have given anything to stay, Leah pushed herself out of Jeremiah's embrace.

"As much as you and I want things to be different, they are not," Leah said finally. "Jeremiah, in some ways, the congregation is right. They wanted you to have someone better than what Secret had to offer. They wanted you to have a Rachel. I'm just a Leah. What you need is a Rachel."

Jeremiah picked up her cold hand and brought it to his warm lips. "I'm afraid I have to disagree. Do you know the genealogy of Jesus?" he wiggled his eyebrows mischievously.

Unsure as to the direction he was going, Leah didn't answer.

"Jesus came through Leah's line, not Rachel's," Jeremiah supplied. "The Jacob of the

Bible thought he needed a Rachel, but the world needed a Leah. For it was from Leah that our Savior came. Maybe the congregation doesn't realize that what they really need is a Leah."

Leah wet her lips, unsure how to respond. Was he really saying that, despite what his parishioners may feel, he still thought that she would make a good pastor's wife? Perhaps more importantly, was he saying that he wanted her to be *his* wife?

"And you?" Leah whispered shyly. "What do you need?"

Jeremiah smiled and, once again, drew her into the warmth of his arms. "That, dear Leah, is the best question you've asked. I already know that the Rachel of my heart, happens to be named Leah. Now I pray that the Leah I want is also the Leah God needs for me."

Leah's heart melted. Could she believe him? With a Miss Hardesty and a Miss Cox, could he really want Leah?

"And if you're still not sure, let me make it very clear how I feel about you. Leah Barton, I—"

"There you are! I've been looking all over town for you!"

Colder than any Sierra wind came a strident voice.

Leah leapt out of Jeremiah's embrace, retreating as far as she could into the bushes and away from the approaching Winifred Beagle.

"Can I help you, Mrs. Beagle?" Jeremiah asked, recovering much more quickly than Leah.

"Where is Miss Hardesty?" she demanded. In the rapidly waning light, Mrs. Beagle glared at Leah as if she had disposed of the other woman in some fiendish manner.

"She left several minutes ago," Jeremiah explained. "She was stopping by the mercantile to pick up your package. She should be arriving at your house for dinner any time now."

"Humph! Mrs. Beagle sniffed. "Well, that's not exactly what I was expecting. I came to fetch Begonia before the snow got worse. I thought you would be escorting her, Reverend Moore. Instead, I find you here. With *her*. I'm sure you were simply discussing the church helping her unfortunate family. But we should always be mindful of appearances."

"Actually, no," Jeremiah shot back with a hard edge to his voice. "Our discussion was more personal in nature, if you must know. I believe a pastor is allowed to have personal discussions that are not the business of the church. Am I correct? But, if it would suit you, Mrs. Beagle, I would very much like to escort you home and discuss a few pressing matters with you." Jeremiah turned to Leah. "Miss Barton, I will look forward to continuing our conversation later. Can I offer you a ride?"

Leah shook her head. "The Tufts' house is only a short distance, and I would prefer to walk. Thank you."

Mrs. Beagle, looking entirely too pleased with herself, allowed Jeremiah to help her up into the wagon seat. "I was expecting that you would seek out my advice on these pressing matters, Reverend Moore. As always, I am happy to offer my wisdom to your needs."

Leah turned to hurry away.

"Oh, Miss Barton!" Mrs. Beagle called.

Leah reluctantly turned back around.

"I was disappointed to find that two eggs were broken when the children delivered them Saturday morning. I was able to salvage them, but they had to be used immediately for Mr. Beagle's breakfast."

"I'm sorry, Mrs. Beagle," Leah said quickly. "I will make sure you have an extra two eggs when I deliver next."

"Well, I suppose that will have to do," Mrs. Beagle replied, obviously reluctant to relinquish her offense. "But if you purpose to keep customers, you should make the deliveries yourself, or provide better instruction and supervision of your siblings. Mr. Beagle says that he watches those brothers of yours skip and run right in front of the bank. How can you expect eggs to stay intact with that kind of behavior? I am not a heartless woman, however, and I have pity for your unfortunate circumstances. Normally, for such an infraction, I would deduct the entire cost of the egg order from my payment. But I know you are dependent on the little egg money you collect, so I will only deduct the cost of the two broken eggs."

With a self-satisfied smile, Mrs. Beagle dismissed her with a regal wave of her hand. In her mind, she had done her civic duty today, providing wisdom on how Leah should conduct herself while also granting mercy and benevolence in the face of an infraction.

Leah didn't look at Jeremiah but turned and hurried away. The snow was falling heavier now, quickly covering her footprints as if they'd never been there. By the time she arrived at the Tuft's house, all traces of her tears were gone as well.

It was all impossible. Jeremiah's promises, his kisses, his spiritual insight—none of it mattered. Mrs. Beagle's treatment said it all. Nothing could change the reality that she was the daughter of the town drunk and someone to be pitied. She was just a Leah. And that would never change.

Chapter 12

"Leah, you look so pretty!" Hazel said sweetly, her bright eyes looking up to her sister.

"Thank you," she said, hanging up her cloak on a hook in the church foyer. "I had no idea Miss Jolly had such nice dresses."

Leah looked down at herself, making sure her skirt was hanging straight. In the bag of clothes Jeremiah had brought her, she had found several beautiful garments. The styles were older, and Jolly had obviously not worn them in a long time. But with a few little tucks here and there, they fit Leah perfectly.

She felt conspicuous as she stood waiting to enter the sanctuary. She certainly had never worn any dress as fine as the soft white she wore now. It was horribly impractical and sure to collect stares, but it was a dress like she'd always wanted. Thinking that such a garment required the rest of her appearance to match, Leah had even attempted to do her hair in a fancy hairstyle she'd seen in one of Mr. Tuft's catalogues. Though others may find her silly, the look of admiration on Hazel's face made Leah happy that she was beautiful to at least one person, even if that person was only four.

Now with all of their coats carefully hung in the church entryway, and the children gathered around her and looking somewhat respectable, she had no more excuses to prolong her entrance.

Except that she didn't want to be here. Jeremiah would announce his decision about the mail order brides in service this morning. Despite what had happened between them, Leah was certain that he should, and he would, choose one of the brides. Leah had not seen him since last Monday when they kissed. She'd heard that he'd been called away to a nearby town for some pastoral duties. She'd also heard that he'd not gone alone. Miss Hardesty had accompanied him.

Jeremiah must have changed his mind. That was the only explanation. Otherwise, he would have sought her out to talk to her again.

And now, she would have to listen to him announce that he had chosen a bride, and that it was not her.

Not that she blamed him. She had given him no reason to hope and no reason to think that she could return his affection. She'd instead given him the opposite. She'd told him it wouldn't work. Jeremiah was right to move on and select a bride from one approved by the congregation.

At least that's what she told herself.

Curtis and Johnny started a shoving match, and Leah knew she could put it off no longer. She could already hear hymns being joyously belted from the pews.

Closing her eyes for two seconds, she breathed deeply and prayed, *Lord, please help me get through this!*

The door opened behind her.

Leah turned to see her father come through the church doors.

Stepping in with a cool gust of outside air, he quickly turned and shut the door behind him.

"I'm sorry I'm late, daughter," Jim Barton said meekly.

Leah's mouth fell open in shock. Her pa had stayed around the house more than usual this week. He'd even brought home some fresh meat that he had actually gone hunting for. But he had still disappeared for long periods. If he was drinking, he was trying to spare Leah by not coming home drunk. This morning, he was nowhere to be found for breakfast, and as this wasn't unusual, Leah hadn't given it a second thought.

Now here he was attending church in his Sunday best, clean but worn clothes that hadn't seen use in at least two years.

And he said he was sorry he was late.

A sob caught in Leah's throat. By the look on his face, Leah knew those few words encompassed so much more than a single Sunday.

Bart stomped last night's fresh snow off his boots and hung up his threadbare coat. Though he was trying to be brave, Leah saw the tension in his jaw and noticed that he couldn't quite manage the confidence to meet her gaze.

Snapping out of her shock, Leah reached for his hand, and the children gathered around him, anxious to proudly walk into church with their pa. Leah knew there would be gasps of shock and those who would be offended by the presence of such a sinner. She also knew that "Bad Bart" still had a long road ahead of him.

But he was in church.

And that was more than enough of a miracle for today.

"Come, daughter," Bart said. "I believe you were right. The good Lord wants me to be more than a drunk. And I aim to figure out what that is!"

Leah's heart skipped.

She knew that many would doubt Bad Bart could change. They would have thought it impossible that he would attend church.

Maybe God was in the business of making impossible things possible.

But if that was true for her father, could it also be true for her?

Was she meant to be more?

On her father's arm, she entered the sanctuary. She heard the gasps and whispers. She saw the startled, and even horrified looks sent their direction.

With head held high, she smiled and walked to a pew halfway up the aisle.

Though they'd entered in between songs, Reverend Moore quickly began another before they were seated.

As he sang the first few words of, "Before the Throne of God Above," Leah looked up at him. She couldn't be sure, but she thought she saw him give a little wink her direction. And his smile was unmistakable.

Leah stifled a giggle. She realized Jeremiah was intentionally taking the focus off her family. It was well-known that Mrs. Beagle quite vocally objected to the church singing this particular hymn. Leah thought it was beautiful, but Mrs. Beagle viewed any hymn written in the last hundred years as horribly modern and therefore sacrilegious.

With those first few words of the song, all eyes in the congregation turned from the Bartons to a very stern-faced Mrs. Beagle. Through every word, the congregation watched as the woman sat with lips pursed in a thin line, refusing to sing a word.

After singing the full three verses with great gusto, Jeremiah concluded the singing and began his sermon. Leah listened carefully as he expounded on his text of Galations 1:10: *"For do I now persuade men, or God? Or do I seek to please men? For if I yet pleased men, I should not be the servant of Christ."*

Though it wasn't a direct lecture on the congregation's behavior, it had definite applications.

It was impossible to not see the correlations when Jeremiah talked about how we should be pleasing God, not man. Leah also couldn't help but apply the text to her own life and Jeremiah's words the other night.

Jeremiah's words from the other night drifted through her head, but they sounded eerily like the same words she'd spoken to her pa. Did she really believe that the only opinion that mattered was God's? If she really did, then she shouldn't care what Mrs. Beagle and the rest of the town thought, right? She shouldn't let them determine who she was. She should trust that God would do what He said and work in her to accomplish His will, even if it was difficult.

She didn't want Jeremiah to marry someone else. The more she watched him, the more she realized that she loved the sincere, intelligent way he delivered his sermons. She loved the way he genuinely cared about others. He wanted to help and didn't mind striking up a conversation with those that others might find objectionable. She loved the way he didn't let Mrs. Beagle intimidate him and met any challenge without flinching. She loved the way he laughed and the way his gray eyes twinkled when he smiled.

She loved him.

If she truly was a servant of God, she shouldn't turn away from something God may be calling her, especially if she turned away because she feared the opinions of others.

And if God called her to be a pastor's wife, to be Jeremiah's wife, what others' thought wouldn't change the fact that she would be a blessed woman indeed.

The jostling of little bodies in the pew beside her roused Leah from her thoughts. Leah looked down to see Johnny and Curtis elbowing each other and fighting over a pencil and... a wanted poster?

"Boys!" Leah hissed, snatching the paper that now featured an outlaw with a carefully drawn handlebar mustache over his lip. Leaning forward, she made a grab for the pencil as well.

"That's mine!" Johnny said, trying to wrench it back out of her fingers.

"Where did you get it?" Leah whispered, wondering who she was going to have to apologize to about her brothers swiping the nice quality pencil.

"Mr. Beagle gave it to us!" Curtis said, looking like he was about to cry about losing the prized possession.

"Mr. Beagle?" Leah asked, thinking she had heard wrong.

"Yes, he always gives us little things if he's outside when we go by the bank. He gave us this pencil and told us if we practiced our numbers, he might give us a job at the bank when we got bigger."

"But we didn't have any paper," Curtis said, his lower lip still trembling in worry that she wasn't going to give back the pencil.

Leah blinked, trying to come to terms with the realization that Mr. Beagle had shown kindness to her brothers for no reason at all. He hadn't done it for show. There had really been no reason. And with the way they spoke, it was apparently not the first time the man had done so. Had she been so focused on Mrs. Beagle's negative behavior that she hadn't noticed Mr. Beagle's consideration?

Glancing from the pencil to the earnest little faces, Leah realized that letting the boys write and draw during the service may not be a bad idea at all.

"I'll let you have it back," she said, but you can't fight over it. You have to take turns."

Both boys eagerly nodded.

The last song finished and with a leap of her heart, she realized that it was time for Jeremiah to make the announcement about the brides. Glancing around, she realized that, during the service, the sanctuary had filled over capacity. Now, the curious, standing-room only crowd eagerly waited to hear which bride the pastor would choose.

And as far as Jeremiah knew, Leah still wanted nothing to do with him.

"Leah, give the pencil back!" Johnny insisted.

Leah looked down at the pencil in her hand and suddenly had an idea.

Curtis elbowed Johnny. "Shhh! Preacher is gonna marry those brides now!"

Though Curtis wasn't accurate in his announcement, it advertised enough excitement for Johnny to immediately forget about the pencil in lieu of the potential of better entertainment.

"I know everyone is awaiting my decision regarding the brides ordered by the congregation," Jeremiah began. "While the congregation's actions were misguided, I can find nothing objectionable about the two women who were deceived into coming here."

Having no time to find a better option, Leah smoothed out the wrinkled Wanted poster and hurriedly wrote across the top, right above the outlaw's picture, three words: Marry me instead.

She didn't allow herself time to change her mind, but jumped to her feet and rushed up to the front. Jeremiah was standing several feet away from the pulpit, but, trying to be unobtrusive, she slid the poster right on top of Jeremiah's Bible, turned, and, with face flaming red, hurried back to her pew.

She caught Jeremiah's look of curiosity, but otherwise didn't even look at him.

Jeremiah walked casually back to the pulpit. He reached for the poster.

"So which 'un are you gonna marry?" Frankie boomed anxiously.

Jeremiah's eyes shot up.

"While both young women are commendable, I must confess my heart has led me in a definite direction, one that I believe the Lord has purposed that I take."

Leah tried to keep breathing. He hadn't read her message! His eyes had drifted down for less than a fraction of a second. Not enough time to read it. And now it was going to be too late!

Leah's gaze swung between Frankie and Mrs. Beagle, seated, quite appropriately, on opposite sides of the sanctuary. Each wore a satisfied smile, as if certain that their choice of bride was clearly the one selected.

The rest of the congregation appeared to be holding its breath, save Curtis and Johnny, who were busy using their chores as currency to make wagers on which bride Reverend Moore would choose.

"I know not all of you will be happy about my choice," Jeremiah ventured. "But I hope and pray that from this day on, you will be supportive and loving, as God would have you. I ask that you please respect my wishes, and seek unity. This is my final decision, and there will be no discussion or trying to convince me otherwise. Finally, I ask that you *never do anything like this again!* I don't want any gifts. If you have a question, or an idea, ask. If you want to surprise someone, don't. If you wonder if someone might be offended by your actions? Don't do it."

Look at the poster! Look at the poster! Leah silently beseeched him.

But he didn't.

His focus stayed on his audience.

Jeremiah paused, gathering himself. The congregation leaned forward, each person seeming to hold his or her breath so there wasn't even a whisper. The air itself was still.

Jeremiah spoke, "I believe that a man should have the right to choose his own wife, even if he is a pastor. That is a personal decision, and while he should try to find a suitable helpmate who would support his ministry, the only ones who should have a vote are him and God."

Jeremiah paused, his eyes sweeping to include every person gathered in rapturous anticipation. "I will not be choosing either of the brides provided by my congregation. I was not consulted or responsible for them being brought here, and I feel it only right that those who are at fault should be held responsible for their welfare. Frankie, you and your group are hereby responsible to provide Miss Amy Cox with boarding until which time you pay for her to go where she wishes, or you honor your original agreement with her and provide a husband that meets with her approval."

Everyone's gaze shifted between Jeremiah to the two women sitting in the front pew. With serene looks on their faces, they were the only people in the room who did not appear surprised.

"We gotta find her a groom?" Frankie asked, eyes wide in horror.

"Yes. And Mrs. Beagle, you will be required to do the same for Miss Begonia Hardesty."

Mrs. Beagle looked as if she'd just tasted something sour, but she said nothing.

"I really don't think it should be a problem," Jeremiah continued. "You didn't seem to have trouble locating a quality bride, you should be able to use those same skills to find a groom. But the stipulation is that he must be approved by the bride, with her full knowledge and consent. Until that time, you must provide for her lodging."

"We'll have to marry her off within the week," Frankie said firmly. "None of us got the money to keep her in the hotel long."

"But, preacher!" Johnny called. "If you ain't gonna marry those brides, who are you gonna marry?"

Though she would likely deny ever agreeing with Johnny Barton, Mrs. Beagle spoke up. "Reverend Moore, I understand that you are offended by our methods, but I beg you to reconsider. Our sentiment is still valid. The town of Secret would like to see you happily settled down with a wife."

"Oh, I never said I wouldn't be getting a wife," Jeremiah said with a smile.

"Who?" Mrs. Beagle asked, clearly confused. "Will you be sending for your own mail order bride?"

"No," Jeremiah replied firmly. "I'll marry Leah Barton instead."

Yet another audible gasp rippled through the church, and all attention turned to Leah.

Her eyes locked with Jeremiah's. Almost as if she was floating, her feet propelled her forward. Jeremiah took hold of her hands securely in his.

"I didn't think you saw my note," she whispered, a little self-conscious about their audience.

"Of course I did. I just didn't have time to give your stationery a closer inspection. I'd already decided to wait for my bride until she was ready, but I'm thrilled I didn't need to wait long."

Leah nodded and smiled shyly. "Thankfully, you won't need to work seven years for your Leah."

Jeremiah laughed. "Praise God for that!"

Turning serious, he looked at the wide-eyed congregation. Apparently deciding to say his peace anyway, he lowered his voice to be heard only by her and brought her fingers to his lips. "Leah, I can't promise what life will bring. We are in Secret, after all." He wiggled his eyebrows and tipped his head to their audience. "But I can promise to love you through whatever comes our way. Leah Barton, would you do me the honor of becoming my wife?"

Leah nodded, "Yes!"

Though they hadn't heard the words, the congregation clearly understood what had just happened. A smattering of applause broke out, very possibly instigated by the jilted brides in the front row. Johnny and Curtis hooted and hollered. And Hazel, having found the welcome arms of Mrs. Tuft, beamed shyly.

"This is not acceptable!" Mrs. Beagle protested with her strident voice cutting through the celebration. "Why she is...! She can't be a preacher's wife. Her father—"

"Has joined us for church this fine morning," Mr. Tuft supplied with a smile. "I'm sure he would be happy to answer any questions you have about his daughter's qualifications."

Mr. Barton stood from his pew proudly. Even the streaks of tears on his face couldn't compromise the air of dignity that surrounded him.

"Mr. Beagle!" Mrs. Beagle sputtered. "Tell them that this won't do! Tell them!"

Responding to his summons, Mr. Beagle also stood from his pew and cleared his throat, as if he actually might speak.

But his wife beat him to it. "Mr. Beagle says—"

A deep, booming voice interrupted. "Mrs. Beagle and I would like to extend our most hearty congratulations to Reverend Moore and Leah Barton," Mr. Beagle said formally. "Miss Barton is a fine young lady, and will make Secret proud as our pastor's wife. Reverend Moore has made an admirable choice, and I couldn't be happier."

"But... but..." Mrs. Beagle stammered, pale with shock.

Despite his formal speech, Mr. Beagle's eyes twinkled, and Leah got the distinct impression that he was thoroughly enjoying his wife's discomfort in the situation.

"Mr. Beagle, that is not what I wished to say!" Mrs. Beagle finally managed.

The rotund man took his wife's arm. "I think you've said quite enough, my dear. Now, if I might escort you home, you have some work to do finding a groom."

Turning to Reverend Moore, he said, "Please let us know when you have a wedding date. I'm sure Mrs. Beagle wants to provide a reception for the town in your honor. She does so enjoy those type of things."

Mrs. Beagle fell mute as Mr. Beagle escorted her out, and the rest of the congregation fell to talking and commenting on the excitement.

Leah looked down at her hands clasped with Jeremiah's. Then she looked back up, trying to communicate without words her love for him and the new peace she felt. God had plans for her, and those plans included Jeremiah.

Here she was, standing beside the pulpit of a small church in the Sierra Mountains, beside a pastor who was to be her husband, with an audience that included her imperfect siblings and father, and serving a cast of characters that could challenge the most devout minister.

Yes, she was exactly where God wanted her.

With a hoot of joy and a fling of his hat, Frankie grabbed all attention.

"We done did it!" he shouted. "We got us a Secret bride!"

Please look for Book 2 in
The Secret Bride Society series

The Secret Bride Ballot

Coming Soon!

Author's Note

When first writing this book, I thought Secret would be a great name for a town. Then I found out that there is (or was) a Secret Town, California. I thought such a real place would be a perfect setting for my story. However, despite my efforts, I could not find much to go on, and most of the information about Secret Town will remain just that—a secret.

What I lacked in nonfiction, I made up for with a whole lot of fiction. I let my imagination build a make-believe town with a real name. Everything that is Secret Town in my book is fictional, but the delightful part is that the little bit I've been able to discover about the real Secret Town fits in perfectly with the imaginary one.

Secret Town, California is the site of a massive railroad trestle that was built for the trans-continental railroad. A simple google search will provide some pretty impressive images of what it looked like. It was a significant feat at the time, a curved railroad trestle 1,100 feet long; but it had an inglorious fate. It was built in a hurry in order that the railroad be completed. My understanding is that sometime later, it was deemed to be unsafe. The massive amount of wood used to construct it had fatal flaws—decay and flammability. Since having a bridge rot or catch fire was not considered to be a good thing, Chinese laborers were then tasked to fill in the Secret Town trestle. Supposedly twelve years after it was built, the beautiful and significant structure was buried and forever relegated to a few photos on a google search.

As to the obvious question of the origin of the Secret Town name, the answer is that no one knows for sure. The theory I like best is that the ravine was named for a company of miners who wanted to conceal their finds of wealth.

So If you are ever in California, traveling along Interstate 80, watch for a sign that says, "Secret Town." I really wish that I could provide a great history and tourist guide for this place with a marvelous name, but I can't. The sign is about all there is.

But now, maybe you can be like me, and that little sign will have much more significance. For, though we'll never know the real Secret Town, we will know the imaginary one. And the pretend Secret is probably way better than any reality could have been anyway.

If you have enjoyed this book,
please help spread the word and leave a review
at your place of purchase!

Other books by Amanda Tru

YESTERDAY series:
Yesterday
The Locket
Today
The Choice
Tomorrow
The Promise
Forever (coming soon)

TRU EXCEPTIONS series:
Baggage Claim
Mirage
Point of Origin
Rogue

BRIDES BY MAIL Series:
(Written with Cami Wesley)
Bride of Pretense
Bride by Request
Bride of Regret

THE SECRET BRIDE SOCIETY Series:
The Secret Bride Society
The Secret Bride Ballot (coming soon)

<u>Christian Romance:</u>
<u>Secret Santa</u>
<u>The Random Acts of Cupid</u>
<u>The Assumption of Guilt</u>
<u>The Christmas Card</u>

<u>Clean Romance:</u>
<u>The Romance of the Sugar Plum Fairy</u>

<u>Children's:</u>
Under the pen name J. Lasterday
<u>DOG THE DRAGON series:</u>
<u>The Dragon's Escape</u>
<u>The Cabin Boy's Treasure</u>

About the Author

Amanda loves to write exciting books with plenty of unexpected twists. She figures she loses so much sleep writing the things, it's only fair she makes readers lose sleep with books they can't put down!

Amanda has always loved reading, and writing books has been a lifelong dream. A vivid imagination helps her write captivating stories in a wide variety of genres. Her current book list includes everything from holiday romances, to action-packed suspense, to a Christian time travel / romance series.

Amanda is a former elementary school teacher who now spends her days being mommy to her four young children and her nights furiously writing. Amanda and her family live in a small Idaho town where the number of cows outnumbers the number of people.

Connect with Amanda Tru
Amanda loves to hear from readers!

Website
http://amandatru.com

Email:
truamanda@gmail.com

Facebook:
https://www.facebook.com/amandatru.author

Twitter
https://twitter.com/TruAmanda

Newsletter Sign up
(sign up to be notified of new releases)
http://eepurl.com/ZQdw9

Sneak Peek
of

Bride of Pretense

(Brides by Mail Book 1)

A Historical Western Christian Romance
Book 1

Chapter 1

St. Louis, Missouri, 1880

ADELAIDE Delaney set her brown floral carpet bag on the bench beside her, hoping it would warn others away. The last thing she needed right now was for some overly friendly person to sit next to her, forcing a conversation.

Having the train delayed was a bad omen. Not that she needed another reason *not* to get on board.

"You don't mind if I sit here, do you?"

Addie was just about to say, yes, I definitely do mind, when the lady lowered herself onto the bench, shoving Addie's bag into her hip.

Addie tried to scoot as far away as possible, but the edge of the bag still bit through her layers of skirts. However, the young woman next to her didn't seem to mind that half of her posterior was positioned atop Addie's carpet bag. Instead, she proceeded to take off her hat and begin fanning herself in the most unladylike fashion.

"It's so hot here, in St. Louis, isn't it?" Not waiting for a response, the woman continued. "Although, I'm from Georgia, where it's even hotter and more humid. Where are you from? I'm Charlotte, by the way. Charlotte Mason from Atlanta, Georgia. What's your name?"

Addie glowered at the young woman seated next to her, or rather on top of her bag. Addie reached between them and grabbed the small leather handles pulling them toward her, away from her unwanted companion. With a solid yank, the bag flew out and hit Addie right on her face.

"I'm so sorry!" Here, let me take your bag for you. There's plenty of room for it under the bench next to mine. There. Now you don't have to hold it. How's your nose?"

"Fine."

Addie turned away from the other girl and took out her handkerchief to delicately dab at her injured nose. Hopefully, Charlotte would take the hint, and refrain from further conversation.

But luck was not with Addie today. Charlotte continued her monologue, not seeming to notice Addie's sideways glares.

"I'm headed to Texas this afternoon to meet my fiancé." Charlotte glanced around discretely before lowering her voice in a conspiratorial whisper. "I haven't actually met him before. I'm a mail order bride."

Addie gaped at Charlotte in surprise. "Wh-what?" Oh, if her tutor, Miss Carrington could hear

Addie now! She would be horrified by her former student's uncultured stuttering. Addie was the daughter of Moses Delaney, the great shipping magnate. She did not stutter.

"Well, I saw an advertisement in the newspaper for a gentleman looking for a bride. He was very specific, saying that she had to be a good Christian girl who could cook, clean, and help with other aspects of farm life. He also required references, which I provided before we began to write letters. His name is Joshua Harding. Isn't that a handsome name?"

Charlotte once again didn't pause for an answer. "He owns a cattle ranch by Austin. He also has pigs, chickens, and a few horses. He doesn't live too close to the nearest town, about an hour's ride, which doesn't bother me because we will have each other, and we got along so wonderfully in our letters. He's simply perfect."

Charlotte paused, her blue eyes gazing off into the distance, a happy smile on her angelic face. She really did resemble an angel with her light blonde hair framing her round face and pale blue eyes. Addie had blonde hair and blue eyes too, but she looked considerably less heavenly.

"What about your family? How do they feel about you leaving your home and moving so far away to marry a stranger?"

A dark shadow passed over Charlotte's face. "I have no family. My pa died when I was little, and Mama just passed away. This is my chance to start over, to belong to someone, and have a family of my own."

"I'm so sorry." Addie regretted inadvertently bringing up a painful subject for Charlotte. Though it seemed the two women shared little in common, Addie knew what it was like to lose someone.

"Don't be," Charlotte said, her smile gently returning. "I know my family is in heaven. I also know that God is providing a new family for me."

"How can you be so sure?" Addie asked, curious in spite of herself. Charlotte seemed so certain, so confident that the train would take her to where she was meant to be. "You've never met this man. How can you know this is what you should do?"

"God told me," Charlotte replied simply.

And with those three little words, Addie immediately disliked Charlotte Mason from Georgia.

Addie held her breath, waiting for Charlotte to continue, to explain what she had meant. But with a serene smile fixed on her face, she now chose to be silent.

Addie clenched the handkerchief in her hand, trying to manage her annoyance. After sitting in the same pew, in the same church, every Sunday for her entire life, Addie had never felt that God had spoken to her directly. Most of the time, she felt like she was pushed around in the dark, sending up prayers that never reached higher than the ceiling. People like Charlotte, who seemed to have everything figured out and confidently 'heard' from God, drew her instant dislike.

Not that Addie should esteem Charlotte. She wasn't exactly of the class with which Addie normally associated. Charlotte's simple brown traveling suit starkly contrasted Addie's elaborate navy one.

Addie reached up and adjusted her hat just a little. It was the newest style and just purchased for this trip. But even the physical reminder of her wealth did nothing to convince Addie that Charlotte didn't have something she longed for.

Finally, unable to take the silence any longer, Addie burst out. "I don't understand when you say, "God told you…"

Charlotte pursed her lips, as if thinking, then finally broke her silence. "Everything happens for a reason. We might not understand God's plan, but He is still in control. You have to go where God leads you, and He will take care of the rest."

"Yes, but how did you know?"

"Well, I prayed and th—" three short blasts from the train halted Charlotte's words. "Oh, no, that's my train! I really want to answer your questions, I sincerely do, I just need to freshen up before boarding. Wait here, and we will talk until I have to leave."

"But—" Addie was so close to getting her answers! Charlotte couldn't leave now! But there she was, bending to search with her fingers for the handles of a carpet bag that looked remarkably familiar.

"Wait!" Addie called, but Charlotte had already disappeared behind the depot doors. Addie glanced under the bench, confirming her suspicions. Charlotte had grabbed Addie's bag by mistake. The carpet bags were similar size and color, Addie could see how in Charlotte's haste she had taken the wrong one. Oh, well, Charlotte would be back soon, and Addie could remedy the situation before Charlotte left for Texas. Addie's train would not be leaving for another hour. She had time to wait.

Addie tapped her pointed boot to the rhythm of seconds ticking by. She stared at the impostor carpet bag beside her, wishing its owner would appear to retrieve it. To Addie, it was almost repulsive. Charlotte's bag looked like a fifty year old version of her own. The attractive brown floral pattern had faded to a muddy swirl, and both the handle and brass clasp looked as if a stiff wind could convince them to abandon their posts.

As the minutes wore on, Addie couldn't tolerate sitting still. Finally, she stood from the bench, snatched the carpet bag handle in her sweaty palm, and walked across the platform toward Charlotte's train. Stopping in the middle of the platform, she turned a full circle, craning her neck in a completely improper fashion, desperately looking for any sign of the missing mail order bride.

The train whistle blew. Startled, Addie jumped, jerking the handle of the carpet bag up sharply. The fragile brass clasp popped open. Addie tried to grab the bag before it upturned, but she only got hold of one side. With the weight of the bag shifting, it teetered. Addie reached for the other end, but couldn't grab it before the entire contents of Charlotte's bag emptied in a flood all over the train platform.

Addie gasped, immediately turning a brilliant shade of crimson at the sight of lady's undergarments spilling around her feet. She quickly bent over, trying to both hide her face and shove Charlotte's possessions back in the bag.

Mens' boots clomped their way across the platform as Addie hurriedly worked. She carefully kept her eyes down to the wayward possessions and the passing feet, never having the nerve to look up at the faces belonging to those shoes, and hoping no one would offer to help.

She stuffed the undergarments in first, followed by Charlotte's now dusty nightgown and night cap. A dress, equally brown and drab as the one Charlotte had been wearing, went in next. A tin of crackers (very likely now crumbs), a still-intact mirror, a sewing kit, and a few other small toiletries were unceremoniously returned to their home. Finally, Addie grabbed Charlotte's heavy Bible and placed it as the crown atop the other possessions.

She started to rise, but then saw a packet of envelopes hiding partially under her skirt. Addie retrieved the papers, intending to toss them on top the Bible, but at the sight of the return address, Last Chance, Texas, she paused.

These were Charlotte's letters from her would-be groom!

Without conscious thought, Addie secured the flimsy carpet bag clasp as best she could and wandered back to the bench, where she sat and stared at the packet in her hands.

Feeling a little guilty, but assuring herself that she would only look to see if Charlotte's train ticket was amongst the papers, Addie undid the neatly tied cornflower blue ribbon binding the envelopes together. Thumbing through, Addie found the ticket at the very back, where Charlotte had obviously slid it in to keep it safe.

Instead of retying the ribbon and replacing the letters in the bag, Addie leafed back through the envelopes, noting that Charlotte's Joshua Harding had a very strong, masculine scrawl.

Now feeling a lot more guilty, Addie watched as her slightly trembling fingers slid out the papers folded neatly in the bottom ivory envelope.

She knew she shouldn't read the letters. That would be very rude and beneath her. She was not a snoop.

Charlotte would be back any minute. How horrible for her to return and find Addie reading through her personal letters from her future groom!

But Charlotte's story and Addie's curiosity won over her better judgement. Addie would just take a little peek. Just to see if Charlotte mentioned how God had spoken to her. Yes, that was what Addie was looking for. Charlotte had said that she really wanted to answer her questions. But that would be impossible now. Charlotte was taking far too long tending to her personal needs.

One letter. That was all. Once Addie made up her mind, she slowly unfolded the paper with her gloved fingers, placing the other envelopes securely in her lap, along with the ticket.

A picture fell out. At the sight of the man's face staring back at her, Addie forgot about the letter. She let the paper drop softly to her lap and held the portrait with both hands. It wasn't a typical portrait. Instead of a suit, Joshua had posed in his ranch clothes and hat that concealed all but a little dark hair peeking from beneath. He looked proud and had a strong, masculine jaw that hinted of stubbornness. Joshua Harding looked every inch a rugged man of the West.

But Addie liked his eyes most. They were honest and kind. Her own fiancé's eyes were cold and devoid of emotion, especially when they looked at her.

With her gloved finger, she gently touched Joshua Harding's face, feeling an intense longing that Charlotte's fiancé was the one meeting her at the end of the line, not her own.

A long train whistle followed by two short ones jarred Addie from the picture.

She looked around frantically. Where was Charlotte? The train was going to leave without her!

She gently laid the picture back in the carpet bag with the others and popped back up off the bench, desperately searching the platform for a hint of Charlotte's blonde hair.

The crowds were larger now as people rushed to their trains. What was she going to do? She didn't have her tickets to Denver. They were tucked into her own carpet bag, the one currently in Charlotte's possession.

Addie pushed her way through the passersby, positioning herself directly in front of the steps to the train. She dug out Charlotte's ticket and gripped it tightly in her hand. When Charlotte came, she would quickly trade her bags and the ticket so the other woman could board quickly.

Charlotte had been gone so long that Addie was now in danger of missing her own train. What if her train left before she found Charlotte? Papa would be so angry.

For a moment the train station melted away, replaced in her mind by another depot. She imagined her train arriving in Denver without her. Addie was a bride-to-be as well. But there was a difference. Charlotte chose to be a bride. Addie was being forced into an arranged marriage with the son of one of her father's business partners.

Well, not partner yet. Addie was being offered as a token gift to seal the profitable partnership between a railroad baron and her father, the merchant. Her father stood to make a great deal of money if Isaac Trenton saw her fit to be a bride for his son, Blake.

Addie was being sent to Denver to be inspected and to determine if she would be suitable. A lot was at stake in this 'business transaction' as Addie's father had told her before sending her out the door and on her way alone to Denver. She was not to fail her father now. It was her responsibility as the only child of Moses Delaney to follow through. After all, she had already failed him by being born a girl.

Addie's thoughts shifted once again to her arrival in Denver. Blake might be there to meet her, but most likely not. She had met him once before in NewYork when he came with his father to discuss terms with Moses. Blake had made it clear then that he didn't want this marriage any more than she did. He would most likely send a servant, if anyone at all to meet her at the station. Addie's arrival would not bring nearly the excitement and anticipation that Charlotte's would in Texas.

The conductor's voice thrust Addie from her painful thoughts.

"Miss, is this your train? Will you be traveling to Texas today? The train is ready to leave."

"No, please wait a few more minutes." Addie paused, searching for a way to describe her association with Charlotte. She racked her mind, but found herself reluctantly saying, "I have my friend's ticket. She should be here any moment."

"We can't wait, Miss." The conductor glanced at his pocket watch. "We have a schedule to keep."

Charlotte was going to miss her train. There would be no mail order bride arriving in Last Chance to meet Joshua Harding. At that moment, Charlotte's words came back to Addie, as if whispered on a welcome breeze. "Everything happens for a reason. We might not understand God's plan, but He is still in control. You have to go where God leads you, and He will take care of the rest." Could this be God's will for Addie?

In one gloved hand, Addie held a ticket to a new life, a chance to get away from her arranged marriage. In her other hand, she carried Charlotte's carpet bag, packed with handwritten letters by a man with kind eyes—a man who wanted a bride, a companion to spend his life with. Not someone who was bound by an arranged marriage. Blake Trenton didn't want a bride. Joshua Harding did.

"Last call, Miss. The train is leaving with or without your friend."

Addie searched the crowds one last time for Charlotte. Seeing no trace of her bench companion, Addie raised her chin a fraction and turned to the train, her mind made up.

"Here's my ticket, sir. I will be going to Texas today."

Bride of Pretense

is available on Amazon, in paperback, and on other major online retailers.